BOOKS BY *AUBREY MENEN*

The Prevalence of Witches
The Stumbling Stone
The Backward Bride
The Duke of Gallodoro
Dead Man in the Silver Market
The Ramayana
The Abode of Love
The Fig Tree
Rome for Ourselves
Speaking the Language Like a Native
SheLa

SHELA

A satire

SheLa

A SATIRE

AUBREY MENEN

RANDOM HOUSE
New York

For Philip Dallas

CONTENTS

Part One	In Nirvana	1
Part Two	Washington	23
Part Three	New York	53
Part Four	Everywhere	89
Part Five	Quarg	123
Part Six	In Nirvana	155
	A Note	195

PART

[1]

IN NIRVANA

[1]

TREMBLING IN EVERY PERFECTLY SHAPED LIMB,
the Angel of the Lord, called Michael, approached
Nirvana, which was about ten-feet square and surrounded by a white fence; on one side of the fence
was a gate with a latch. In the middle of the en-
closure was a tree with drooping branches. The
tree was transparent. Under the tree sat Prince Sid-
dhartha, known as the Buddha. When the Buddha
was angry, which was almost all the time, the tree
glowed red. When the Buddha was peaceable, it
shone with a cool blue light. The tree was now

scarlet, and the nearer the angel approached to Nirvana, the redder it grew.

The Angel Michael folded his wings. Timidly, he raised the latch of the gate.

"Have you no manners?" roared the Buddha. "Knock before you enter, and wait till I ask you. And do not," said the Buddha, as the angel prepared to do as he was told, "do *not* knock too loud. I have no patience with insolent flunkeys."

"No, Your Highness," said Michael.

"Nor with your insufferable Master," added the Buddha, flashing his eyes. He was a tall spare man, brown, with a bold hooked nose and long gray hair. His eyes were extraordinarily piercing.

"Quite so, Your Highness," said the Archangel. He knocked gently on the gate.

"You may come in. Close the gate after you."

The Archangel entered. He carefully refastened the latch, drew himself up in a military fashion and saluted. "Praised be the Lord of Hosts," he said.

"Not here, he won't be," said Buddha. "You are standing on territory that has been free, independent and democratic for three thousand years. Take off your helmet and sit down."

The angel did as he was bidden.

"There," said the Buddha. He smiled. His smile was of great charm, in spite of being underneath so prominent a nose. "You couldn't do that in front of His Omniscience, could you? How does it feel?"

The angel smiled back. "There's nothing a soldier likes as much as taking the weight off his feet," he said.

The Buddha looked at the angel more closely. "Ah," he said, "you're Michael, aren't you? Excellent! You're a good lad. I like you. You're not like the others. You have a mind of your own."

"Don't say that, sir," said Michael. "You'll be getting me into trouble."

"Trouble, eh? What will the old tyrant charge you with. Dumb insolence?"

"Something like that, sir. It means five minutes' LK in front of the troops."

"LK? What's that? Ah," said the Buddha, "I understand. Five minutes' Loving Kindness, eh? What's it like?"

"Very lowering, sir." Michael looked about nervously, peering into the blue beyond the white railings. "I really shouldn't be talking like this," he said.

"Don't worry," said the Buddha. "He won't hear you. It was part of the bargain over extraterritorial rights."

"You don't say!" said Michael. "I always understood that he was omno . . . omni . . ."

"Omniscient," said Gautama. "Everywhere but between these fences. He capitulated after my first thousand years of meditation. I'd more or less discovered what your C-in-C was up to. He bawled and thundered a bit, but when I threatened to be reincarnated in my own person and go down to earth and tell the whole suffering, deluded race of guinea pigs we call human beings, he capitulated. I was given Nirvana," he said, sweeping his hand in a gesture round his tiny domain, "and I promised to meditate two more millennia." The Buddha took a bag of dates and a bottle from behind the tree, which now glowed a tranquil blue. "Have something to eat and drink."

"Thank you very much, sir, but we're not supposed to accept offerings," said Michael. But he eyed the bottle and the bag wistfully.

"And what about the C-in-C?" said the Buddha. "Does he?"

"I should say he was very partial to them," Michael replied. He took the bag and opened it. "Dates, aren't they, sir?" The Buddha nodded. "I've seen human beings eat. I've often wondered what it was like."

"Very nice," said the Buddha. "One thing that really upset your C-in-C's reckoning was that I discovered a way of not eating for a whole year and still won every argument I had with him."

[6]

"Nice, you say, sir?" said Michael. He shook the bottle. "But aren't the after-effects a bit . . . well, you know, sir, not nice at all."

"They're quite disgusting. That is one of the reasons I gave it up. It offended my sense of decency. I resented being made to do such revolting things at your C-in-C's command. Why not try the experiment? It will give you some idea of His Omniscience's vulgar sense of humor."

"I will, sir," said Michael. He cautiously tried a date and then a little from the bottle. "Very good," he said, wiping his lips with the back of his hand, "very good indeed."

The Buddha watched him for a while. Then he said, "Tell me, Michael, is this the first time you've eaten food?"

"Yes sir," said Michael, with his mouth full.

"You've never felt hungry?"

"I beg your pardon, sir—I don't quite follow you."

"Of course you don't. You've never felt hungry. Nor tired, I suppose?"

"No, sir."

"What keeps you going, Michael?"

Michael, who was drinking from the bottle, put it down and wiped his lips with the back of his hand. "It says in the Regulations that we are kept going by the light of His countenance, Your Highness."

"The light of His *what?*" said the Buddha.

"Countenance, sir."

"Those are the very words?"

"Know the whole book off by heart, sir," said Michael, munching a date. "Those are the very words."

"What vanity! What egoism! What sickening self-satisfaction! But apart from the purple prose, Michael, you must admit it is a clear, simple, orderly arrangement. Your C-in-C wants you to exist, so you do. When he doesn't . . ."

"Phht," said Michael.

"Exactly. But supposing the arrangement were this: in order to exist you had to eat one of the Cherubims. Further, you had to digest him with a corrosive fluid and dispose of him in an unmentionable manner. The Cherubims, in their turn, had to eat and dispose of an angel a day. The angels, in order to be nice and plump for the Cherubims, had to eat smaller angels, and these had to gobble up the still smaller ones who sing soprano in the heavenly choir. Imagine, too, that the heavenly choir did the same thing, the basses ate the altos, and the altos ate the trebles. What would you think of it?"

Michael took another date. He frowned with

mental effort. "Ah!" he said. "I see what you're getting at, sir. What would the trebles eat? That's what's worrying you, isn't it, sir?"

"No, you idiot."

"Just as you say, sir," said Michael.

"Don't get into a huff, Michael."

"I'm not in a huff, begging your pardon, sir."

"You *are*, Michael," said the Buddha. The tree behind him changed from crimson to a color near purple.

"No, sir, I'm not, sir. There's no need at all to excite yourself. I'm merely . . ."

"I am *not* excited, Michael. I am *never* excited. Are you aware that on earth millions of people burn incense to statues of me just because I am famous for never, never, never losing my temper but always preserving the most *absolute* calm?"

"A very creditable reputation to have, sir. It just seems to me, sir, that thinking about those altos eating the trebles and so on catches you on the raw."

"It does, Michael."

"And I can see your point, sir."

"Thank you."

"It certainly does seem a long supply line, and that's a thing I never did hold with."

"It is a preposterous supply line, Michael. It is a monstrous supply line. It is the most cruel,

[9]

perverted and sinister supply line that could possibly be imagined. And your Commander-in-Chief imagined it, out of his own free will. When I discovered the whole grotesque story, I determined for the sake of the dignity of my fellow human beings that I would discover a way of escaping from our ludicrous and bloody destiny. I did. But unfortunately it was so difficult that nobody but myself could follow it. But I am proud to say that every so often some bold spirit arrives who has a good try."

"Well, sir," said Michael. "I'm a simple soldier. And, in the course of my duties, I've had the privilege of talking to many other simple soldiers down below, sir—in their last moments they're very partial to a prayer or two to me. It's been my experience, sir, that it's better for a simple soldier not to think too much about what goes on in General Headquarters. It's inclined to be discouraging. Better do your duty and leave it at that. Which reminds me that I am instructed to deliver a message to Your Highness."

"From him?"

"Yes, sir."

"I've said it before and I'll say it a thousand times again, I want no dealings with intermediaries. I demand a meeting at the summit. Nothing less. I am perfectly well aware of the fact that he doesn't want to see me for the very good reason that, on the one and only occasion we met face to face, I got the better of the argument."

"So I've heard said, sir."

"*Have* you?" said the Buddha, obviously pleased.

"It was much talked about at the time, sir, until it was declared an official secret. Be sure I'll take your message back to the proper quarter, sir. Meantime, if you'd be so kind as to let me deliver mine, you'll be doing me a favor. I shall be able to return in good order—mission completed, and so on. I'm sure you'll understand, sir."

"Very well. What is it?"

"I am to inform you, sir, that the new Dalai Lama has been found."

"What of it?" said the Buddha, contemptuously. "It was once a good idea of mine. But it didn't work. The lads get into the hands of a lot of idiotic priests who fill them up with bunkum. Your master knows that perfectly well. Why should he bother to send you with such idle information?"

"I don't know, sir. He impressed upon me that you were to be told, whatever the difficulties you put in the way. As it turned out, I've found the task easy, not to say pleasant," said Michael, raising the bottle.

"I suspect a trick," said the Buddha. "I've

been expecting one ever since I discovered the latest abominable jest which His Ineffable Mightiness intends to play on suffering humanity. And *that*, let me tell you, Michael, is one so malicious it could have been thought of by the Devil himself, if he hadn't muddled his wits with thinking too much about sex."

"Talking of the Devil," said a mild and deprecating voice, "may I come in?"

"Ah," said the Buddha. "You."

"Yes, me," said the Devil. He was standing a little behind the back part of the fence, in a modest and self-effacing posture.

"By all means, come in," said the Buddha. "Any member of the opposition is always welcome here, as you well know. But I beg of you, none of those interminable dirty stories you are so fond of."

The Devil held up his hand. "I promise you faithfully, not one. I heard your remark to Michael about it. I deserve your rebuke. It's just that moving about in my profession—and I'm interested in my work, very—moving about, as I say . . . Well," he said, with a little laugh, "I admit that I am too inclined to the professional failing of thinking that there's nothing like leather. And," he said, as he walked around the fence, "there isn't."

The Devil unlatched the gate. The Archangel

Michael got to his feet. "I must be going. Two's company."

The Buddha rose. "Why don't you stay, Michael? Finish your wine and listen to our conversation. It might broaden your mind."

"That's just what I'm afraid of, sir."

The Devil came into the compound, a slim, spare man, sporting the small beard and disordered hair that is usually affected by defeated revolutionaries. "Spoken like a soldier," said the Devil, with an affable smile. Turning to the Buddha, he added, "And a very good soldier, too, I may say. When Michael and I had that little showdown, he beat me fair and square. I was routed."

"Not before you gave me some pretty bad moments," said Michael, putting on his helmet. "You had me guessing several times."

"That's handsome of you, Michael," said the Devil. "But the fact is I was out-generaled."

"Well, I don't know," Michael replied. "I'm not sure there's much in generalship. It's just the trick of being on the side of the big battalions, or running away with dignity if you aren't. Brains don't count. It's the stuff the troops are made of. Yours were damned good, if I may say so. There was just one thing wrong with them."

"And what was that?" asked the Devil.

"They had a cause, and they thought their cause was just."

"Bravo!" said the Buddha. "Well said."

"And that," Michael proceeded, "is a very unsettling thing for a soldier. As I've said to my men many a time, a soldier doesn't have to know right from wrong; as long as he knows right from left, he'll do fine. Which reminds me, it's time I got back to duty."

Michael drew himself up. "Gentlemen," he said, and saluted. He turned on his heel and walked away a step or two. Then he stopped, squared his shoulders and said in firm military tone, "Alleluia." With that, he left them.

The Buddha gestured to the Devil to sit down, and he himself resumed his place under the tree, which now shone a peaceful blue.

"You can't help admiring him," said the Devil, looking in the direction of that part of the sky into which Michael had disappeared. "So bluff, so blunt, so manly."

"Too much so," said the Buddha. "I was trying to get him drunk to see what he would be like. But you came in before he'd finished the bottle."

"I'm sorry," said the Devil. "It was an interesting notion of yours. Yes, of course, he overdoes it. But you cannot really blame him. One of the Master's little jokes was to create his angels in the image of human beings, except for one thing. When it came to making them either men or women, he stopped short and made them neither. I have often wondered why."

"A piece of pure irresponsibility, I should imagine," said the Buddha. "He had probably set himself the problem of creating an ideal staff of domestic servants. Have you never thought of asking him directly, face to face?"

"Yes," said the Devil. Then he made a gesture of despair. "But . . . well, you know yourself."

"I do," said the Buddha. "He would beg the question." He changed his voice so that it became portentous. " 'Thou asketh me why I have created the angels neither man nor woman. Go thou and tell me why I gave the ape a blue behind.' "

"You catch the spirit admirably, Your Highness. Do you know, I have often wondered that if the truth were known we wouldn't find out that the one we're dealing with isn't just a petty official. He speaks so like one. A petty official with wide temporary powers."

"I'm sure of it," said the Buddha. "I am by nature a deeply religious man. I seek something in the universe to revere, to love with all my heart and soul. I shall find him. He exists. But to find him I must penetrate through this illusion, this charlatanry with which we are surrounded. That is why I am called the Enlightened One, or, in less fancy language, the One Who Was Not Fooled."

"Conversation with you is always so refreshing," said the Devil smoothly; but the Buddha replied, "I have civilly invited you into my compound. You might at least spare me your bedside manner."

"I beg your pardon, of course," said the Devil, abashed.

"Tell me," said the Buddha. "Does this trick about having no sex apply to you?"

"Unfortunately, yes. As an archangel," said the Devil, "it could scarcely be otherwise. But I incline rather to the feminine side."

"I see," said the Buddha. "Is that why you take so much pleasure in prying into people's private affairs?"

"I had never thought of it that way, but it could very well be so, Your Highness."

"I cannot imagine how you can go on doing it," said the Buddha. "I was, indeed, as you call me, a Highness. I was a Prince who loved his subjects and found them so perfectly disgusting in their habits that, duty bound, I went off into the jungle to think of something better for them to do with their lives. I may say that I found it. I showed them the eightfold path to rising above their squalid selves. I do not say I was fully understood.

But, on the other hand, what I taught has never been forgotten."

"You have made a signal contribution to elevating the human race and, in case you want to snap my head off again for paying you compliments, allow me to say that, in my own modest way, I think I have done the same thing."

"How? By encouraging people to do things their better selves tell them they shouldn't?"

"Like you, I am much misunderstood. I do not encourage. I tempt. I tempt people to do things that their better selves tell them they could not possibly dream of doing. I have no interest in people who feel themselves wicked. I am fascinated, on the other hand, by people who are sure that they are good. I set them a little trap to prove to them that they are not. It is very salutary. A clear-headed man like yourself will admit that if it were not for the Devil there would be a good deal more hypocrisy in the world than there is. As I always say, think what conceited opinions people would have of themselves if it were not for the Devil."

The Buddha sighed. "You have a roundabout mind—as roundabout as your Master's. No doubt that is why he got rid of you."

"He certainly has no fondness for brains of any sort in his entourage," said the Devil. "Do you know why he has so many musicians around him?

[17]

It's because it's the one profession where you **can** rise to the top and still be as stupid as an ox."

The Buddha ignored this and went on with what he had been saying. "Besides, what are these suggestions you make when you test somebody? The temptations of the flesh? Psha! You encourage your victims to immorality, but morality itself is nothing but making a mountain out of a mole-hill. There is no need of it. You do not need an elaborate code of regulations to keep down the temptations of the flesh. They can be conquered by ten minutes' clear thinking. I've done it, so I know. You have merely to go off to some quiet place and sit under a shady tree. There you contemplate the plain, simple, undeniable fact that if the Creator had wanted, he could have made all living things produce themselves as simply as a crystal grows in a solution. Instead, we are saddled with this unclean, ridiculous, upsetting, inefficient, inelegant, and often unsuccessful system of the mating of the sexes: a thing . . ." he said warningly, as he saw the Devil about to speak, "which, by definition, you know absolutely nothing about. That, no doubt, is why you can never tear yourself away from the subject. To proceed: once anybody has grasped the truth about this indecent jest, he has merely to decide whether he will go on being a clown or give up the whole thing in the name of his self-respect. For me, there was no choice."

"Your austerities made history," said the Devil.

"My common sense made history," said the Buddha.

"If only you could have discovered the way for human beings to propagate themselves like— what is it? Crystals," said the Devil.

"Since you know perfectly well I did not, you are suggesting that I am talking nonsense, I suppose?"

"Far from it. I think you are quite right," said the Devil eagerly. "The present system is full of absurdities. Some of them, as you say, are comical. I am reminded of an instance that came my way recently. There was a young woman . . ."

The Buddha's tree flared crimson and the Devil, observing this, trailed off into silence. Then he said, "As you were saying—crystals . . ."

"Nobody but a fool and the perpetrator of the jape could find the predicament of human beings funny."

"No, Your Highness."

"No doubt if I were to tell you the last and final trick which is to be played, you would burst your sides laughing. So I shall not tell you. I shall merely inform you that I intend to fight it. I intend to warn humanity of its peril. I shall strengthen it in its hour of trial. I am, at this moment, looking for someone who will be my messenger, my mouthpiece, my representative among men at the hour of their greatest trial."

The Buddha ceased speaking. His eyes blazed. For a while he seemed unaware of the presence of his visitor. Then, as the tree faded into more tranquil hues, he said, "I am in no mood, I am afraid, for your flippancies. Please state your business with me as briefly as possible and then be so kind as to leave me."

"Certainly," said the Devil humbly. "It was just that I . . . and this touches, perhaps, on your mission—your noble mission to humanity, with which I wholly concur, although you have not as yet told me, honored me with—"

"Come to the point!" snapped the Buddha.

"I wanted to ask Your Highness whether you would be interested to know that the Dalai Lama . . ."

"He has been found," said the Buddha. "Michael told me."

"So I overheard," said the Devil.

"Well?" said the Buddha, since the Devil showed no signs of going.

"The Dalai Lama is, I understand," said the Devil, "supposed to be your living representative?"

"It was an experiment. It invariably fails."

"I see," said the Devil. "Then you won't be interested in my news."

"I have already heard it."

"Not quite. Michael was perhaps a little confused by the wine, but I feel he did not deliver the whole of his message. Then again, his Master may have held back part of it. As you say, one must always suspect a trick."

"What part?" said the Buddha.

"This," said the Devil, enjoying his triumph. "There is not one new Dalai Lama. There are two."

"*Two?*" said the Buddha. He was utterly astonished, and that, as the Devil remarked on his return to his headquarters, was a sight worth seeing.

PART

[2]

WASHINGTON

[2]

GEORGE TRUNDLE, ON THE OTHER HAND, WAS AS-
tonished by nothing, except perhaps the fact that
after seven disastrous years he was still the principal Adviser on Foreign Affairs to the President of
the United States. The President had appointed
him to his post during his first week in office. Now
the President was nearing the end of his second
term, and George Trundle was still at his post and
still trusted. He had been appointed not because
he had any great knowledge of foreign countries
but because he had brains and a prolonged education. Long residence in several of the best Ameri-

can universities had made him an expert in academic administration. He had buckled down to his new and strange job; seven years later he was still buckling down, but foreign affairs were to George Trundle as foreign as ever.

Yet the President's faith in him was unshaken. The President believed firmly in brains. As he himself had said, "What else have we got to think with?" Trundle's enemies in the administration had been known to suggest that George might try a ouija board, but after the most tremendous of George's blunders they were driven to conclude that he had taken their advice.

George worked in a small office in one of the adjuncts to the White House, and he worked very hard. He was a small, neat man in his forties, with carefully combed hair and bright eyes that flashed knowingly behind academically heavy spectacles. These eyes were the only notable feature in his face, but they were striking. Whenever George made a very great mental effort, they watered slightly, giving him an expression of vivid intelligence. George was an absolutely sincere man. When he was asked a question to which he did not know the answer, he tried very hard to think one up. His eyes suffused; his questioner would go away (when, that is, George had learned the simple trick of keeping his mouth shut) impressed with the fact that Trundle knew a good deal more than Trundle was prepared to say.

But this gift of George's would not have been enough by itself to impress the President. The President, too, had an intensely intelligent look, so he knew its worth. George had a more valuable virtue. After a prolonged study of the way that the men in charge of foreign countries behave, he had hit upon a profound truth: When they acted, they did so without a thought of the effect that they would have on local American political elections. When, for instance, one of them hanged the outgoing chief minister, he did so without so much as a passing thought for the impending gubernatorial race in, say, California.

Every so often, George Trundle made so bold as to tell this to the President, and the President was grateful for it. "George," he used to say, "in my position I have to take the broad view. I have to concentrate on the important things. A man like you is invaluable to me, because you show me the significant detail that I might have overlooked."

George treasured this remark. The President had made it at the time when another head of state in Southeast Asia had refused to postpone a war until after the senatorial elections. The President had threatened to cut off American aid—not because of the war, which he thought justified, but because of the timing, which he considered a gratuitous insult. George had been able to prove that the head of state in question knew nothing of the elections, being convinced that the Senate was appointed in the same manner as he appointed his own.

George read diligently every report that was put in front of him but, like television news announcers, he did not find this practice very much help in understanding what was going on. Still, he was always abreast of events and, provided nobody asked him to give a lead, it was a creditable position to be in. Moreover, when things went wrong, as the President's Adviser on Foreign Affairs he always readily took the blame, but when things went right he never claimed any credit. This endeared him to the President.

The world is a big place and each day a formidable stream of information was placed on Trundle's desk. It would have dismayed many a man, but Trundle's academic background saw him through. With scholarly precision, he would note down on a piece of foolscap all the names of persons and places. He would then summon his assistants and between them they would get the pronunciation right. This took a lot of time, but it was worth it at the subsequent conferences with the

President. When everybody was losing their heads over the name of some new African secessionist, Trundle would come out with it, clear as a bell.

But on the day when the news of the two Dalai Lamas came on George's desk, this system did not work. None of his assistants was an authority on Tibetans, and the only reliable book in the section had been borrowed by one of the typists, who had developed an interest in mysticism. A wrangle broke out. The typist, in tears, was sent home to retrieve the book, but before she got back Trundle was summoned to the White House. Feeling unsure of himself, he determined to pass over the matter lightly, should he be asked.

The President was in an affable mood. An election* in New Jersey was going unexpectedly well. He greeted George warmly. An enormous blunder of George's had caused, it was true, the United States to be humiliatingly defeated at the United Nations. The morning newspapers had called for Trundle's head on a charger, but mildly, like a man who asks for a dish he fears is out of season—after all, they had asked for George's head

* The President was an Eisenhower-Democrat. He was opposed by the Roosevelt-Republicans. Non-American readers should remember that these two parties were formed after the second campaign of Mr. J. F. Kennedy, when it was found that the programmes of the two traditional parties did not show enough difference to make a fight of it.

half-a-dozen times before and never got it. Besides, the President's popularity polls had risen sharply. Nobody had quite explained why, but cynics had suggested that Trundle, when doing his worst, called out all the latent optimism in the American people.

There were about eight people at the meeting, all sitting informally, if uncomfortably, on chairs of period design, except the President who sat in a more commodious chair. The current run of affairs was discussed briskly for a while. Trundle was called upon to report on certain matters which were under, as the President was fond of saying, review. Trundle kept them there. Then, as usual, the President said, "And is there anything new, George?"

George cleared his throat, and said, "There's this about two Dalai Lamas, but . . ."

The telephone rang at this point. The President eagerly snatched up the receiver. From his expression, it was clear that New Jersey was doing very well indeed. A long conversation took place, at the end of which the President, beaming, relayed the news to the company. A most animated and happy discussion broke out. It might have gone on for a long time, but the President was the master of the situation. He raised his hand and, with a pleasing smile, brought the group to order.

"And now back to your llamas, George," he said. "Two, you say?"

Everybody, including George, marveled at the way the President could hold so many things in his head at the same time. "Yes, Mr. President," said George. "One has just been chosen by the Communists, but another, I'm glad to say, has already been chosen by the Free Tibetans—a refugee group in . . . ah . . . a refugee group . . ." said George, since the actual place had slipped his memory.

"I see," said the President. "Do you think we should take any action?"

"Beyond lending our support to . . ."

"The free one," said the President. "We shall do that. These might seem small affairs to us, but they carry great weight in . . . in, where did you say, George?"

"Yes, they do," said George. "Yes." He squinted down at his papers. Fortunately, at this moment a very tall and large man came into the room. With a manner surprisingly soft for so big a person, he mumbled an excuse for being late.

"Never mind, Tod," said the President. "We've just reached a point where there's something for you. There are—correct me if I am wrong, George—two llamas. One free. One Communist. It's the very thing for you to handle."

[31]

"Yes," said Tod, sitting gingerly on a small chair. "It is, isn't it? Llamas," he said, his voice fading away.

Tod agreed in this way with practically everything said to him, for he did not feel his position in the Administration was a particularly strong one. But he was a Presidential favorite. A writer by profession, he had been called in to warm up the public image of the President. His job was to portray the Chief Executive as a man who did not allow the cares of State to take up all his day but, on the contrary, would always find time for small, human actions. The campaign had been an enormous success with the public, who to Tod's puzzlement seemed eager to believe that the President was not earning his salary.

"We, of course," said the President, "back the free llama. What shall we do, Tod?"

"Llamas," said Tod. "Let me see. Llamas. We could find a mate perhaps from among our Latin American friends."

"Excellent," said the President.

George said, "Yes, but I mean . . ."

Tod, mild as he was, could be stubborn with opposition. "It went very well with that seal," he said.

The telephone rang again. The President seized it. He listened and gave a jubilant cry. New

Jersey, it was clear, was in the bag. When he re-
placed the receiver another lively discussion broke
out. After a while, the President glanced at his
watch. He rose briskly to his feet. He laid a hand
on George's shoulder.

"Those animals," he said. "Have a word with
Tod, will you, about them. Sacred animals can
catch the public imagination, especially in the
East."

"Mr. President," said George, "they are
men."

"Not sacred llamas, then?" said the President.
"Not the ones I was thinking of?"

"No," said George. "Men." He looked very
white. "That is," he said, holding up the paper,
which he had at last found time to read. "One is a
man. The other—the other, Mr. President, has
turned out to be a woman."

The President was still master of the situation.
"Which one?" he demanded keenly.

"Ours," said Trundle. "Unfortunately."

The matter might never have been heard of
again in Washington had the President been a
lesser man. But the President's extraordinary mind
never stopped working or rather "reacting," as he
preferred to call the process. In the case of the
Dalai Lamas, he did not react until later that
morning while taking two minutes off from meet-

ing his advisers in order to answer a call of nature. In those two minutes—often so idly passed by the rest of us—the President reacted—the President mentally catalogued everything in this fashion— (a) to the fact that the toilet had at last been repapered in a design of wallpaper exactly contemporary with the date of the installation of the plumbing; (b) that he was to meet the Russian Ambassador Tschempko at three P.M.; (c) Tschempko was a Communist; (d) what had he heard new about communism that morning? (e) the Dalai Lama; (f) the Dalai Lama was something to do with Indochina? Hyderabad? Tibet? (g) it was Tibet; (h) Tibet was Communist.

The moment that he was once more at his desk he reached for the telephone and asked for the State Department. "Get me," he said, "the Buddhist desk."

At the Buddhist desk William Weekly let the instrument ring for a while, convinced that the caller was his wife. This was likely, because for six months nobody else had rung him at all. Then, with a sigh, he took up the receiver in his long, scholar's fingers and put it to his delicately shaped ear. An expression of controlled despair settled on his face, that had grown pale in the best libraries of the Western world.

"This is the President," said a manly, forth-right voice. "To whom am I speaking?"

"William . . ." said Weekly, and was quite unable to finish his name.

"It's like this, Bill," said the President, with his habitual promptness of mind. "I'm in need—but quickly—of some up-to-date information about the Dalai Lama, or Lamas, as I understand the situation to be as of now; and everyone here tells me you're just the man to give it to me—Bill," he added, in his most friendly tone of voice.

The warmth of the President's voice ran through Bill's veins and revived him. He had waited a long time for this moment, and he screwed himself up to rise to it. He was a man who knew his job. Five years of postgraduate study at Harvard and the Sorbonne had rendered him a master of the French language and culture. Told that the State Department had its eye on him, three more years spent at Yale had rendered him an expert in Russian affairs. Snapped up by the State Department, he had been given a post almost immediately as the vice-consul in the small Italian port of Civitavecchia, where he stayed for another seven years, signing visas for seamen. Unnerved, he had thrown himself into the study of Sanscrit in order to keep his reason. After a nervous break-down he was transferred, in the same grade, to the

even smaller Italian port of Leghorn, where he
added Pali to his linguistic accomplishments. This
had landed him, after another year, at the Buddhist desk in the State Department in Washington,
where now the President of the United States was
speaking to him in person. It was, after all, a great
career.

"You already seem very well informed, sir,"
said Weekly. "There are, indeed, two Dalai
Lamas."

"I'm fairly abreast, Bill," said the President.
"But what I want you to do is to give me the thinking behind this thing."

"Well, Mr. President, it's this way," said
Weekly. "The new Dalai Lama is chosen by show-
ing him a number of things which belonged to
the old one, together with things that didn't. If he
picks rightly, he's considered the Living Buddha.
The Communists in Lhasa have found a nineteen-
year-old boy who's done what's called for."

"Why did they do that, Bill?"

"It's an answer to the growing religious freedom in Russia, sir."

"I don't follow."

"It is a bit complex, sir," said Weekly, rashly
allowing a scholar's condescension to creep into his
voice.

The President grew a shade sharp in tone.

"Don't simplify it for me, Bill," he said. "Give me the facts, and I'll be able to follow you."

Weekly, abashed, went on hurriedly. "Strictly speaking, sir, the Buddhists don't believe in God. Not as you might say the Pope or the Grand Mufti does. It is a nihilistic faith."

"Quite," said the President. "Go on."

"Then again, the Panchen Lama has shown signs of being a deviationist from the Communist party line."

"I get it," said the President. "This is that other Lama."

"Not exactly. He's a sort of Cardinal. The other Dalai Lama was found some years ago in Switzerland."

"My God," said the President, with a groan.

"Yes, sir, it is a bit confus— I mean, Mr. President, it's rather unexpected . . ."

"Switzerland," said the President firmly. "Continue, Bill."

"You see, sir, when the Communists took over Tibet there were a lot of refugees, and a group of them were settled in Switzerland, where the climate and the heights were what they needed."

"Were *we* behind that move?" asked the President.

[37]

"I don't think we ever heard of it, sir. But I daresay we paid the costs."

"Will you check that later, Bill, and let me know? Meantime, tell me about the other Lama."

"One of the priests kept some of the old Lama's personal belongings. He showed them to several boys and one of them picked lucky. The priest told a few people about it, but the Swiss authorities told him to shut up. The Living Buddha wasn't sufficiently neutral for their liking. But he told the Red Cross and the thing leaked. Still, nobody took much notice until the Commies suddenly came up with *their* Lama. The Swiss one is about the same age as theirs, only . . ."

"He's a girl," said the President.

Weekly gasped. "I'm overwhelmed, sir," he said. "So you've actually read my *aide-mémoire* on it? I thought nobody . . ."

"Why do you think I'm on the phone to you, Bill?" said the President in a kindly voice. On a scratch pad on the Presidential desk, he wrote *Budd. desk. Bill who??*

"Thank you, sir. Thank you very much. Yes. It turned out that this boy was a girl. They dress very much alike when young, and her mother thought she'd have a better chance of earning a living. But it appears the girl got sick of it, and when she was old enough to know her own mind she took off her trousers and put on a skirt."

"Philosophically speaking, Bill, is that a heresy?"

Weekly hesitated. "All I can say to that, sir, is that you've asked a very, very good question."

"And here's another, Bill. Does it matter? I mean all this, does it matter?"

Words formed on Weekly's lips: Not a tuppenny damn, Mr. President, not a tinker's cuss.

But he did not say them. He thought of his wife and three children. He thought of how she had dreamed of being the wife of an ambassador when she married him. He thought of his meager salary and lack of allowances in Washington. He remembered Civitavecchia. All in all, his brain worked almost as nimbly as the President's.

"I can't hear you, Bill," said that great man.

"I think it matters very much indeed," said William, firmly. "Buddhism is a branch of Hinduism, and one-fifth of the human race follows that religion. Mostly uncommitted."

"Ah," said the President, and Weekly knew he had rung a bell.

"Woman or not, we've got to remember that in India women have the vote," said Weekly, now inspired.

"They *have*?" said the President.

"Woman or not," William went on smoothly,

"the Dalai Lama in Switzerland is in the free world. The other is in the slave. If I may make so bold as to say so, sir, I don't think there can be any doubt as to where we stand."

The President reflected rapidly. Words leapt into his mind: a) uncommitted; b) free world; c) slave world; d) the woman's vote in India.

"No, Bill," he said, in that tone of authority which he rarely used but always to great effect. "There is no doubt whatever. Thank you, Bill, and I look forward to those checking points I mentioned. Rush them to me personally." The President rang off.

"Yes, Mr. President," William breathed. Reverently he put the receiver back in its cradle.

Washington is the capital city of an open society. It is difficult to keep secrets there, and there is no urgent desire to do so. This is especially so in foreign affairs. The nation, it is true, has sometimes been kept in the dark about policy in this field, but this was only when the President and the Secretary of State were as much in the dark as the public.

But in the case of the two Dalai Lamas the President's policy was clear, and in an hour it was all over town. Political commentators, in particular, hastened to their desks to make a column while the sun shone. They were aware that if things followed their normal course, the President's bold and dramatic decision—characteristic of the man —would be modified under the pressure of events and the Dalai Lamas would pass into the limbo of being under constant and careful review. This partial demise usually took place when Trundle had got going, and normally this took time.

But Trundle could act quickly when he chose, as in the famous instance when, on his advice, the Marines were landed in South America to support an insurrection two whole days before it broke out —a statesmanlike show of force which fortunately turned out to be bloodless because the insurrection failed entirely to materialize. He acted as quickly in the affair of the Lamas.

He telephoned William Weekly and asked him to let him have the briefing that the President had asked for within the next sixty minutes. He then called the appointments secretary and asked for the President's program. As he had expected, a few minutes later a Presidential aide called him in turn and asked for a brief briefing on the situation as soon as possible, since the President wanted to have it in reserve for the afternoon's meeting with Tschempko. All that Trundle now had to decide was how brief the brief briefing had to be. For that he had the facts on his jotting pad.

According to the appointments secretary, from the moment of speaking to one o'clock, the President was in conference with the Senate Floor Leader of his party. At 1 P.M., he was to have an informal luncheon with some minor visiting Arabian royalty. From 2:15 to 2:30, the President would repose. At 2:35, the President was due to make an unscheduled and accidental encounter with members of a women's organization from his home state, who would be making a private tour of inspection of the improvements to the ground floor of the White House. While protesting that he must get away, he would good-humoredly linger until 2:55, when he would be hustled away. At 3 P.M., he would meet Tschempko.

But Trundle knew that the actual talking would not begin until 3:05. Tschempko and the President had met eleven times. A custom had grown up for both men to observe this interval in silence, or chatting with the interpreter after shaking hands. It was a matter of national prestige, neither statesman being willing to give the impression that his side was eager for the meeting. In these five minutes, Trundle calculated that the President could read his briefing if it were confined to one hundred well-chosen words.

It had not always been like this. There was a famous story concerning the President before he

came to office. He was fighting an election for the
Senate. There was some doubt as to the attitude
of a key town, and his party organization had sent
down thirty investigators who made a ten-page report of advice. The President had ignored it and
taken the opposite course to the one they recom-
mended. The President proved right. Asked how he
had managed this feat, he answered, "I asked my
cousin Tom to spend an hour in the drugstore. You
see, he *knows* the place. He was born and bred
there."

It was natural that when he came to office, the
President should prefer the same way of getting
his information about foreign parts. But he was
told that this would not do. A person who was bred
and born in a foreign place would be most unreliable. He would have ties. He would have loyalties,
maybe not those preferred by the Administration.
Anything he said would have to be carefully evalu-
ated. There would be imponderables, and factors,
and such. Whereas a man from Washington who
had never seen the place before would report exactly what he found.

The President agreed with this reasoning, pre-
disposed as he was by nature towards reasoning of
any nature. Plans were made to send people on
missions. People were sent. Unfortunately, they
were mostly people who had to be got away from

their Washington desk by hook or by crook before their incompetence ruined the country, and their reports were thus very varying in quality. So in the end the President was forced to rely on the system of briefings from the Department of State and such new growths as Trundle's organization. With these, suitably condensed, he steered his country through the maelstrom of world affairs.

William Weekly, during his rebellious years as vice-consul, had once come across a pile of briefings with the final brief briefing attached. Having no visas to sign, he attempted to boil down the railway timetable of the trains from Civitavecchia to Rome, on the same system. Having eliminated all small country stations, all slow trains, all special trains and all trains running at unusual hours, he arrived at a brief condensation of the gist of the timetable, which consisted of one train a day, and omitted, for brevity, that it ran at totally different hours between July and September. Taking home this cynical memorandum, he said to his wife that the resulting brief brief timetable was excellent for an occasional traveler but would not be, perhaps, the best basis for a stationmaster to run the railway. His wife replied tartly that if he went on any more like that they would land up for life in Addis Ababa. He had agreed with this and now put in his reports with good grace along with all the rest.

That afternoon between 3:00 and 3:05, the President read Trundle's one hundred words, just as Trundle had predicted. This done, he signaled that the meeting might begin. Here again, custom had its way. Having tried speaking simultaneously, the two statesmen had finally agreed, in separate sessions with the tactful interpreter, that it would be better if they took it in turns, meeting by meeting, to say the first words. The friendly habit had grown up of having the interpreter silently point to the statesman due to open, much in the manner that the Speaker of the English House of Commons inaugurates a session.

Tschempko was a short, heavy man of remarkable ugliness. He had been appointed a special ambassador, not because of his knowledge of international affairs, about which he knew and cared very little, but for the gift he had for making the most simple remark sound offensive. It had long been clear to both governments that there was nothing more to say on any of the issues between them. The balance was perfect. The danger was that one side or the other would make a serious concession and thus re-open the discussions. Since discussions had proved dangerous, in that they might lead to war, a new form of dialogue had to be invented. This had been done and both men were now able to exchange views in the manner of jugglers tossing Indian clubs at each other, the motion being continuous without either man getting hit. To liven the proceedings (much as jugglers toss an occasional club through their crotches) there was the additional aim of provoking one side or the other into saying something silly. Much propaganda could come from this, and no harm be done.

The conversation on this afternoon took, therefore, its prescribed course. Such issues as the destruction of nuclear weapons, the barring of armaments, the dismounting of bases, the stopping of five small but violent wars going on at the time, together with the trading of imprisoned spies, cardinals and such were dealt with deftly. Nobody, so to speak, dropped a single Indian club. During all this, both the President and Tschempko were alert for anything foolish that might be said. The President, in this, was at a disadvantage. He had only his brains with which to entrap his opponent, or, at least, usually it was so. Tschempko, on the other hand, had his aggressive eyebrows, his ugly face and his extraordinarily insulting manner of talking. He was, in fact, an amiable man. But he had been brought up in Soviet Azerbaijan, in a village where polish in conversation was considered a mark of an inherited inability to make successful love to women. He had no such disability, and his brusqueness showed it.

In the early meetings, Tschempko had done well. The President had been prodded into making three incautious remarks and he had thought of breaking off the negotiations. But things had gone better than he expected. His words had been spread over the headlines of the newspapers in the Communist world. But, at home, they had been attributed to Trundle. In a subsequent poll, the President's popularity had once more risen. He continued with the talks.

The last topic of the afternoon was now reached. It was the admission of Communist China to an international body, which the United States firmly opposed. Tschempko opened the subject with the remark that he had studied the latest arguments of the United States. This was merely a statement of fact, but Tschempko's manner of making it was that of an insolent schoolmaster taking a boy's essay between thumb and forefinger, with the words, "I have received this effusion."

The President flushed slightly. Each statesman had two aides sitting behind. One of these men on the President's side noted the flush and coughed. The President turned. The aide bent his glance significantly towards the paper before the Chief of State. The President followed his glance.

He saw Trundle's brief briefing. He smiled. He turned his attention back to Tschempko, who was saying what the President had heard several times before, but even more sneeringly. The President heard him out patiently.

Then the President said, "As I think I have said to you before, Mr. Tschempko, it has been my personal hope that there would be some improvement in our relations with the Chinese government, some basis of good will on which we could build. Unfortunately, there has been no gesture in our direction. None whatever. In fact," he continued, "I am personally sorry to say that the prospect for the future is that our points of view will diverge even further."

He paused for the interpreter to finish this part of his remarks. Then he said, "In the matter of the Dalai Lama, for instance, the United States finds itself firmly, and without hesitation, on the lady's side."

Tschempko gave a long, derisive sniff and noisily cleared his throat. The aides behind the President bent forward eagerly. This revolting practice of Tschempko had disgusted the President until his aides had pointed out that it was an infallible sign that Tschempko was in a corner.

Tschempko leaned back in his chair and put the tips of his thick fingers together. This put his right ear at a convenient distance for his aide to bend forward and whisper. But on this occasion nothing happened. Tschempko bent a little further back. Still there was no whisper. Tschempko sniffed again. He realized he was on his own.

"Mr. President," he said, "my Government has long had occasion to admire, reluctantly, the espionage of the United States. I need scarcely refer to the remarkable photographs secured by Powers on the occasion of his illegal and criminal flight over our territory. But I must say that if you have discovered that the Dalai Lama is not a man but a woman, your photographic apparatus must have been greatly improved. The atmosphere over Tibet is exceptionally clear, of course, but . . . ," he said, and smiled as rudely as he knew.

Both of the President's aides covered their mouths with their hands. They had him. It was plain that Tschempko had not the ghost of an idea of what the President was talking about.

At this moment, Tschempko saw with relief that his aide had slipped a folded note onto his blotting pad. This would be the clue for what he had to say next. Tschempko straightened up in his chair.

The President was speaking again. "We came by our information by the most orthodox channels, I can assure you," he said.

Tschempko got his fingers on the note. "We will probably disagree as to the nature of orthodoxy, Mr. President," he said. "But that need not detain us. Since you wish to discuss the subject, I am willing to do so as far as I can without further instructions."

"I am much obliged," said the President. "We regard the matter as having considerable significance in the overall pattern of our relations with your ally."

The interpreter translated this. Meanwhile Tschempko unfolded the note. It read: *"Sorry. Gone to check up. Back in ten minutes."* Tschempko folded the note and thrust it into his pocket. He turned brusquely towards the aide on his left, but one glance at the young man's rounded eyes and half-open mouth told him that he could expect no help from there. He glanced at his watch. He could break up the meeting on the grounds that he needed instructions. But he had been ordered to keep the encounter going at all costs. He squared his shoulders.

"You're aware," he said, in his rudest voice, "that the Dalai Lama is a religious figure?"

"I am," said the President. "She is."

"I am not a religious man myself. I could wish that the whole system of thinking were done away with. In time it will be. But I would hesitate before heaping vile insults on a person genuinely revered by millions of people."

"That does you credit, Mr. Tschempko," said the President. "So would I."

"In that case, it is difficult for me to understand why you are ready to lend the weight of your great authority to what would appear to be no more than a slander—an obscene slander. The Dalai Lama is a man, Mr. President."

"I fully understand your position, Mr. Tschempko," the President replied. "You must support the contention of your ally, at least until, as sometimes happens, you decide not to. But according to us, the Dalai Lama is a woman. And it is precisely in the name of those believing millions that we lend our support to what you, sir, describe as an obscenity, but which I prefer to call a part of that eternal but mysterious truth which is shared by all religions."

"Yet it would seem to me, Mr. President," said Tschempko, raising his voice a little, "that your professed reverence for the mysterious truth is no more than a cover for a propaganda trick to discredit a devoted man to whom the Chinese Communist Party have, with a broadness of mind that is to be admired, lent their support."

"We, for our part," said the President, with simplicity, "do not need broadness of mind to acknowledge freedom of belief. It is part of our very being."

"Then I may take it," said Tschempko, "that this is the considered attitude of your government."

"You may," said the President.

"And you are prepared to make this base thing public?"

"At the first opportunity," said the President. "In fact . . ." He paused and re-read Trundle's last thirty words of his brief briefing. "We propose to present Her Holiness, the Dalai Lama, before the United Nations, should she agree to detach herself from her religious duties long enough for us to do so."

Tschempko threw in his hand. "I must refer the matter to my government for instructions," he said. Then, as he feared, the President rose to put an end to the meeting. He would have done the same in his place.

The President turned to his aides in the corridor, beaming. "I wouldn't have gone quite so far if it weren't for the fact that I'd got Tschempko on the run," he said. "Ring Kenneth, will you?" he added. "This will look well in the papers, after we've done a little work together on it."

And thus began Trundle's biggest blunder of all.

PART

[3]

NEW YORK

[3]

CABLES NOW BEGAN TO BE EXCHANGED BETWEEN the State Department and its embassy in Switzerland, the contents of which were adroitly leaked to trusted correspondents of the newspapers, who made the most of them. But to the surprise of the White House, the thing hung fire with the American public for several days. Then a cable clerk of Trundle's hit upon a happy idea. It turned out that both the Dalai Lamas had jaw-breaking names that were constantly being corrupted in transmission. The clerk invented a simple code. He called one of them *SheLama* and the other *HeLama*. This was further shortened into *SheLa* and *HeLa*. The State Department is a connoisseur of such devices and immediately adopted the nicknames for its memoranda. In this way, the two names made their way into the press and the headlines. The public was immediately interested.

The previous apathy had not been due to isolationism or indifference. The American public was by now mature. It was fully aware of its duty as a democracy to consider international issues. But it insisted on being an informed democracy. It wanted to know what the issues were. In the matter of the two Lamas, the code names helped considerably. SheLa had the sound of a charming feminine name; HeLa had undertones of a person with low moral principles, if any at all. The issue being thus clarified, the public was immediately united behind the President. People were not surprised to find that the photographs of HeLa, when at last they were obtained by way of Albania, showed a lad who had the appearance of being little more than a gorgeously berobed puppet. As for SheLa, she was seen to be more attractive—in a Tibetan way. Her arrival in New York was eagerly awaited.

Trundle and the State Department had both expected some difficulty in persuading Her Holiness to uproot herself and cross the Atlantic, and considerable teleprinter and cable time was used up suggesting a suitable approach. Trundle was therefore agreeably surprised when he received a telegram of acceptance signed by Her Holiness herself.

It ran: READY TO DEPART SOONEST CABLE AD-VANCE EXPENSES AMEXCO HERE SELF SUITE EIGHT PERSONS FIRST FIRST CLASS BOTH WAYS AWAIT YOUR PROPOSALS ACCOMMODATIONWISE. The cable was date-lined from Rome. Her Holiness, it was clear, was accustomed to American ways. A long despatch from the American Ambassador to Italy explained why this was so.

SheLa, it appeared, was now about twenty. For the last ten years, she had lived at the expense of a rich American widow. She had been dis-covered by the widow in her village in Switzerland, and when (as we have seen) the federal govern-ment of that country began to show signs of dis-pleasure at having a Dalai Lama in their midst, the widow had adopted the child. From then on, SheLa had been given every luxury, including that of a first-class education.

The widow was Mrs. Hamilton Bitney. Mrs. Bitney lived six months of the year in San Diego and the other six months in the Absolute. She had a profound interest in every form of Oriental mys-ticism. She had advised her husband to stand on his head, naked, every morning before going to the office, and he loyally followed her counsel until the day of his death—and, indeed, on it. Dying of a burst blood vessel in the brain, he went into the Realm of Knowing at the early age of fifty-two, leaving behind the gross material trappings of his flesh and five million dollars.

Mrs. Hamilton Bitney was the sole inheritor of this fortune. Her husband urged her in his will to pursue her researches into the Infinite and, particularly, to practice these exercises which, he maintained, had done him no end of good. She was to do them each morning in his memory.

Dutifully, she did so, and this only increased her dedication to her pursuit. She traveled much in the East. She went, as she said, as the humblest of humble *chelas* (disciples). But she was soon known throughout the Orient. Her name passed from monastery to hermitage, from hermitage to ashram, and on many a long dusty road in India, Burma and places beyond, holy men mingled the name of Mrs. Hamilton Bitney with their prayers.

She was nothing if not thorough. She took the vows of a Buddhist nun in a monastery high in the foothills of the Himalayas and there she spared herself none of the austerities proper to the rule. But in three weeks her health showed signs of failing. The Abbess released her from her vows, gently advising her to recuperate at her villa in San Diego and to come back when the southwest monsoon had ceased blowing. Thus was set the pattern of Mrs. Hamilton Bitney's tranquil and dedicated life: half the year in *maya,* or illusion, as represented by Southern California; the other half in reality, as a pilgrim from one Buddhist center to another—for the Abbess, at the urgent request of her coreligionists, had advised Mrs. Bitney to travel widely. It was in this way that the discovery of the Dalai Lama among the Tibetan refugees in Switzerland came to her ears.

Mrs. Bitney had visited the village and been entranced by the "boy," who was very pretty. When the Swiss government threatened to turn the "boy" out, "he" had expressed a desire to live in Rome, where Mrs. Bitney had one of her many apartments.

The idea had appealed to Mrs. Bitney. Rome had the Pope of one religion; it intrigued Mrs. Bitney to give it the Pope of another. Besides, the "boy" had a certain domineering trait in "his" character, proper, no doubt, to the head of a faith.

The "boy" was installed in Rome. The police made inquiries, then difficulties. According to the Lateran Treaties with the Vatican, it appeared the "boy" could not be seen in the streets in the vestments of an alien faith. Mrs. Bitney was told that her protégé could have a permit to stay only if "he" promised to wear normal clothing when in the open.

It was then that the "boy," modestly unwilling to wear Western trousers, revealed that "he" was a girl. Mrs. Bitney was delighted because she had no particular liking for teen-age boys. Besides, as she said, sex was one of the principal illusions of *maya*. In the Absolute, there was no distinction between "he" and "she"; how could there be, Mrs. Bitney argued, when everybody knew that in the Absolute there wasn't even any distinction between This and That?

So she bought SheLa several outfits of feminine clothing and sent her to the International College at Perugia to finish her education. It was there that the American ambassadors to Switzerland and Italy had, by a joint effort, found her.

Accommodationwise, the State Department chose the Saint James' Hotel on Fifth Avenue and 55th Street. There, in the so-called Princes' Suite, SheLa lay sleeping tranquilly on the night of her arrival. All had gone well. She had traveled in robes and one of her suite had held an honorific umbrella over her head at the airport for the photographers. The hotel had lived up to its reputation for being able to cope with all comers. A private elevator had been hung with saffron banners, the Princes' Suite had been dotted with incense burners, and in each of the white and gold rooms a large Tibetan painting of a Buddha had been hung on the wall.

The one in SheLa's bedroom was life-size and very old, so old that its colors had faded. They now faded still more as Gautama Buddha himself slowly took the place of the painted image. He softened his usually severe expression to match the smile of the painting, placed his hand in the Earth-Witness position, and when he had made sure he was suitably awe-inspiring, he allowed himself to materialize. When all three dimensions had been filled, he produced an aura, slowly increasing its intensity until it lit the whole room and set the great crystal chandelier that hung from the ceiling dancing with innumerable colors.

SheLa lay on her bed dressed in a pretty nightgown she had bought in a shop near the Spanish Steps in Rome. Because of the unfamiliar steam heat, she had thrown off the covers and they were piled in a heap at the foot of the bed. Close to her, on her pillow, was a large woolly, spotted toy dog, which had accompanied her in bed ever since she was thirteen. Her black hair was still braided, for she had been too tired to comb it out. She had been beautiful as a child, and she had kept much the same sort of good looks as she had grown older.

She was small in stature and slightly built. Buddha, looking at her with his now fully materialized eyes, thought she looked younger than he had expected from the Devil's description. Still, he determined to go through with his plan. He had made up his mind to tell the Dalai Lama the last and most tremendous secret of what the Deity had in store for the human race and, through him, to call mankind to battle. That he had learned from the Devil that there were two Dalai Lamas made no difference. He would tell both. That one was a woman made no difference, either. The Enlightened One fully agreed with the reasoning of Mrs. Hamilton Bitney.

The light in the room from the Buddha's aura slowly woke Her Holiness. She blinked her eyes and then, with a petulant fling, buried her head in a pillow. A moment later, she turned over quickly in the bed, like a kitten rolling on a carpet. She ended up on her back staring at the Buddha as he sat surrounded by the border of the wall painting. He watched her, silently complimenting himself on having chosen so delicate and effective a way of appearing to her.

Her Holiness stared. Her Holiness rolled over again in the bed until she came in reach of the telephone. She lifted it, glancing back at the Buddha.

The operator answered.

[62]

"This is the Dalai Lama," said SheLa.

"Yes, Your Holiness."

"Am I awake?"

"Your Holiness?"

"I said, 'Am I awake?' "

The night operators of the Saint James' have a world-wide reputation for unfailing efficiency. Smoothly the woman said, "If Your Holiness will take Your Holiness' forearm between finger and thumb and pinch Your Holiness, Your Holiness can find out."

"All right," said SheLa. "Hold the line." She pinched herself.

"Oo," she said. "Thank you."

"You're welcome," said the operator.

SheLa put back the receiver. She looked at the dog. She spoke to it. "Ananda," she said.

Now Ananda is one of the innumerable names of the Buddha, so Gautama answered from the wall, "What?"

"You're welcome," said SheLa. "Do you think she always, *always*, says it? Supposing I'd said, 'I've pinched myself and feel nothing, so I must be asleep. Thank you.' Would she have said, 'You're welcome'? Bet she would have. Isn't it wonderful, Ananda?"

"What?" said the Buddha.

[63]

"Fool dog," said SheLa, rolling back across the bed. "Isn't it wonderful that we're actually in America at last. Ananda, bark, bark, wow-wow-wow-wow-wow . . ."

"Me?" said the Buddha.

"Bark because we're in America and then go and be a brave watchdog and bite that man in the room, because there *is* one, Ananda," said SheLa. She looked with a steady and unafraid gaze at the Buddha.

Buddha smiled benignly. "Do not be afraid, my child," he said.

"I'm not in the least afraid and I'm not a child," said SheLa. She stood the dog on its legs. "Ananda—seize him," she said. "Seize him, boy!"

She surveyed Gautama again. "If you're a thief, I'd better tell you that all that stuff on the dressing table is fake Tibetan jewelry and isn't worth a hundred dollars."

"I am not a thief," said Gautama gently.

"Oo!" said SheLa. "Then you're a reporter. How clever of you to get in that way. I shall give you an interview. I expected to have to give one at the airport, but those dreary State Department people wouldn't let me speak to anyone. Well," she said, propping herself up on the pillows, "this is Ananda. Ananda, say, 'How do you do?' to the reporter. Would you," she said to Gautama, "like to take a picture? One like this," she said, holding the dog up to her cheek.

"I am not a photographer," said Gautama.

"No?" replied SheLa, in a disappointed voice. "What a pity. It would have made such a good picture. I dread to think of the one they're going to print tomorrow in the newspapers. What with the robes and the umbrella, I shall look like Madame Butterfly caught in the rain. Well, if you're not a reporter and you're not a thief, who are you?"

"Gautama Buddha," said Gautama, in a solemn and melodious voice.

"Oh," said SheLa. "Oh yes? Well, I suppose you might be at that. Would you mind very much, though, if I asked you to prove it? I mean, it's late at night and . . ."

"By all means, I shall prove it. How shall I convince you?" said Gautama.

"Your aura. Can you change colors with it?"

The room glowed with all the colors of the spectrum in quick succession and then settled to a steady, lambent gold.

SheLa sighed. "Ah well," she said. "I suppose you must be. Such a pity Mrs. Hamilton Bitney isn't here. It's the sort of thing that interests her very much." She smiled at the Buddha hopefully. "She's on the floor below. I suppose you wouldn't . . ." She trailed off. "No. I see you wouldn't." She sighed again. She put the woolly dog on the pillow and patted it. "You can go to sleep now, Ananda. We're back on religion again."

There was a silence for a while, then SheLa said brightly, "Is this your first visit to New York?"

"*What?*" said Gautama.

"I merely asked, 'Is this your first visit to New York?' You mustn't bite my head off. I was only making conversation."

"This *is* my first visit to New York," said the Buddha obligingly.

"Mine, too," said SheLa and bounced out of bed. "Isn't it exciting?" She ran to the window and tugged at a cord. The curtains drew back, revealing a wide window. Outside, in the night, the skyline of the city glowed and flashed. "Beautiful!" said SheLa. "Beautiful! And to think that tomorrow I shall go shopping down Fifth Avenue."

"And to think," said Gautama severely, "that I have crossed the universe to exchange chit-chat with a scatter-brained frivolous girl. Do you realize who I am?"

"Yes," said SheLa. "I should, after all, shouldn't I? I've been in this thing since I was ten."

"Have you no sense of reverence, you silly girl?"

"No." SheLa paused. She looked straight at the Buddha. "Had you, when you were on earth?"

[66]

The Buddha did not answer for a while. Then he said, "None whatever. But how did you know?"

"Well," said SheLa, "I know a good deal about you. After all, as I said, 'I've been in this . . .'"

"Yes," said the Buddha. "I understood you when you said it first."

"So I know what you did down here. You couldn't have had any reverence for your father, could you, because you walked out on him and went to the forest. You couldn't have had any reverence for the priests, either, because you didn't believe in their religion. And you couldn't have had much reverence for the gods either because you went to an awful lot of trouble to find out what they were all about and you didn't stop till you'd got the truth. It doesn't add up to a very respectful yes-sir, no-sir sort of person does it? I reckon you were a bit of a rebel," she said.

"I was the greatest rebel in the history of the world," said the Buddha. "And I still am." His voice rolled and bounced round the bedroom.

SheLa laughed. "Hush," she said. "You'll wake Ananda."

"I'm sorry," said the Buddha, lowering his voice. "I was carried away by what you said."

"You're impressed, aren't you?" said SheLa,

sitting on the bed again. "Don't be *too* impressed," said SheLa.

"Why?" said the Buddha curiously. "It seems to me that you have an exceptional grasp of what I was thinking in my terrestrial period. Very few people have understood me as well as you have."

SheLa played for a moment with one of her braids. "How long is it since you last talked to a woman?" she asked.

The Buddha hesitated. "Years," he said. "Centuries, perhaps. Indeed, it must be over two millennia."

"So I should think," said SheLa. "You're sweet."

"It is much more than two millennia since anybody has been so impertinent as to call me that," said Gautama.

"But you *are.* Fancy you not knowing that any woman can make a nice little speech like the one I made at the drop of a man's hat. She tells the man exactly what he wants to hear and"—she snapped her fingers—"she's got him eating out of her hand. What a lot you don't know—or, I mean, what a lot you've forgotten in two millennia."

"What a lot *you* have learned in two decades," said Gautama in his most princely style. "It is two, if I am not mistaken?"

"Yes. I'm twenty. But there you go admiring

me again. You shouldn't. Do you know what I'm thinking about now?"

"Presumably you're thinking about women," said the Buddha, "in order to instruct me."

"I'm thinking about *this* woman," said SheLa, pointing to herself. "That's our trouble. I'm thinking that if this ever-so-interesting conversation goes on much longer, I shall have to put some cream on my face, otherwise tomorrow morning I shall look as though I've seen a ghost."

"In a way, you have," said the Buddha. "And, besides, a little frivolity does no harm in a young woman."

"Spoken like a ghost who hasn't dealt with one for two thousand years. A *little* frivolity does no harm. Men like it. They think it charming. But when it goes on, day after day, week after week, year after year, they begin to think it's mental deficiency, and it is," said SheLa.

"You are very severe on your own sex," said Gautama. "Why?"

"Because I've been both a boy and a girl. Most women spend their lives seeing nothing beyond the ends of their noses reflected in the dressing-table mirror. I can see all round the question. My mother brought me up as a boy. But Mrs. Hamilton Bitney preferred girls, and I knew it, so I told the truth to please her, the old bitch."

[69]

"Who is Mrs. Hamilton Bitney?"

"She's the woman who rescued me from that God-forsaken Swiss village where we'd been interned, and gave me everything my heart could desire, except a trip to America which she said would spoil me, and we," she said, hugging the woolly dog, "we jolly well hope it will, don't we, Ananda?"

"If Mrs. Hamilton Bitney has lavished so much kindness on you, I do not think you should call her a bitch," said Gautama.

SheLa rolled over on the bed again, holding Ananda up above her at arms' length. "Shouldn't I?" she said. "What do you think, Ananda? Should we call old Hammy Bits a bitch? No. Perhaps we shouldn't. We mustn't bite the hand that feeds us biscuits, must we? But oh!" she said, throwing down the dog, "that woman is nuts."

"What does that mean?" Gautama asked.

"It means she's nuts. Nutty," said SheLa. She sat up. She tapped her forehead, twiddled her finger and whistled. "Completely, irretrievably nutty. She goes flitting from monastery to monastery and ashram to ashram twirling praying-wheels and looking for the Absolute. What she'd do with it if she found it *I* don't know. She's got five million dollars as it is. Oo!" she said, looking up at the Buddha. "I forgot. Of course I don't know how all this pilgriming would look from your point of view. Different, I suppose?"

The Buddha sat in an inscrutable silence for a while. "No," he said. "From my point of view, it looks nutty. But it took me one thousand years of meditation to discover it, and I cannot help feeling, young woman, that you are jumping to conclusions. But, to borrow your words once again, I can see all round the question. And I must tell you that Mrs. Hamilton Bitney is not *irretrievably* nutty. Besides, what have you got against monasteries?"

"First," said SheLa promptly, "the food. And secondly, the sanitation."

"You should not attach so much importance to the first. As to the sanitation, when a number of people are gathered together under one roof, for however lofty a purpose, that always is a problem. It grew quite acute in my time. But I withdrew to another plane and, until you reminded me, I had quite forgotten the matter."

SheLa got up. She walked over to the dressing table and looked at her face in the mirror. "Tell me," she said. "Did you really withdraw to another plane?"

"Yes."

"Out of it all?"

"Yes."

"To think?"

"Yes."

SheLa turned away from the mirror. She shivered a little as she did so, in spite of the heating. She pulled her nightgown close to her, then found a wrap and put it over her shoulders. She stood by the window, looking at the prospect of the city. "I've lived a funny life," she said. Then, suddenly, "No! This is my first night in New York and you're not going to spoil it for me."

"It's mine, too," said Gautama.

"So it is." She moved from the window and she stood opposite the Buddha. The golden light fell on her face as she stared at him, thoughtfully. "You know, I've never believed all this nonsense about being a reincarnation. I think it began as a trick to make the priests important. Then when Hammy Bits came along, it turned into a gold mine. Still . . ."

"Still what?" said Gautama.

"You're who you say you are, you know."

"Yes, I am."

"I've often thought . . ."

"I know. About the dress you're going to buy tomorrow on Fifth Avenue, and that you've got to put some cream on. What else, my child?"

"If I were to ask you a straight question, would you give me a straight answer?"

"I would."

"Promise?" she said, crossing her fingers.

"I promise."

"Cross your fingers like mine."

Gautama obeyed.

"This Absolute. What is it?"

"It is Everything. It is Nothing," said the Buddha. "It is This and it is That. But it is not This and it is not That."

SheLa stamped her foot and turned away. "I *knew* you wouldn't," she said. "And you *promised*."

"Ah," said Gautama, smiling benignly. "But when I answered . . ." he held up his hands, "I didn't have my fingers crossed."

"Oh!" said SheLa in a fury. She ran to the bed and threw herself full length on it. She buried her face in the woolly dog.

"Are you crying?" said Gautama.

"Yes," she said. "Because I've made a damned fool of myself."

The Buddha stepped down from the platform on which he had been sitting. He came majestically to her bedside. He towered over her, ablaze with light. "My child," he said. "You have been less of a fool than any inquirer after the truth that I can remember. I shall reward you. I cannot tell you what is the Absolute, because that is a silly word invented by ignoramuses to conceal their stupidity. But I can tell you the most important secret in the universe, and that is what I came here to do. I am pleased with you, my child, very pleased. Dry your eyes and listen. And Ananda can listen with you, for this concerns the whole world—even dogs.

"You will know that when, as a young man, I first saw a corpse, I wept. But what you do not know is that they were tears of rage, for it seemed to me a cruel joke that a man full of life and movement should be reduced to a pile of dust. I made up my mind to find a way to release humanity from this preposterous destiny. But I did not know the cream of the joke. I do now. It is this. The life in the man that I saw on the ground was made up of the very dust—of that same dead dust —as the dead earth around it.

"I have, unfortunately," said the Buddha, "a philosophical turn of mind. This makes it difficult for me to understand scientific matters, and, indeed, in my time there were none. Besides, I find some of the long words that scientists are prone to using are very ugly, and I cannot pronounce them with any ease. In my own teachings, I was always careful to use only mellifluous words and simple sentences. That is why some of my teaching is still remembered, though rarely understood. It was, I think I may claim, poetry.

[74]

Science is jargon. But, in substance, the thing that I have to tell you is this. Every thing alive has come from an egg. In that egg is dust, and dust, as I have said, which is not alive but dead. This dust is arranged in a certain pattern, and that pattern determines whether the egg will become an insect, or a dog, or you, or any other living thing that you could name. The arrangement of the dust, and that alone, causes you to be beautiful and intelligent and Mrs. Hamilton Bitney to be, as you say, nutty. The way the dust is piled up determines what the living being shall be, exactly as the way the sawdust is arranged in Ananda determines that he shall look like a dog. There is no escaping from this rule.

"You will now readily see the jest. Mankind is about to discover exactly what makes up this dust —what sort of dead dust put in which order makes a philosopher or a spider, a sinner or a saint, or an octopus. That is to say," said the Buddha, raising a finger, "somebody, who is what he is because of dust, will discover that same dust which makes him what he is. He will—and mark what I say carefully —discover the arrangement of the dust which has made it inevitable that he is the human being who will discover the dust's arrangement. Do you understand me?"

"I think I do, but I'd follow you better if you weren't so fixed on being poetic," said SheLa, who by this time had dried her eyes and was listening intently. "You couldn't give me just one clue in scientific language, could you?"

"No," said the Buddha decisively. "Let us preserve the decencies even when we are talking of so unnatural a topic. This man and thousands like him will be in the unhappy—the tragic position of knowing that knowledge is nothing."

"Please," said SheLa, "I'll put up with poetry, but I refuse to try to follow This-ing and That-ing. Save that for Mrs. Hamilton Bitney. But if I really follow you, then, what you mean to say is that it's like Ananda becoming a real live dog only so that he can understand that he isn't a real live dog at all, but made of sawdust."

"You have stated the matter to perfection."

"What a dirty trick that would be to play on a nice dog like Ananda!"

"Perfection again. You have gone to the heart of the matter. It is a *very* dirty trick, so dirty that it should not be played on a dog, not even a stuffed one, much less a human being. I shall now go on," said the Buddha, "to tell you the result that will follow the jest. I did not imagine that I would come to it so quickly, but you have a remarkably sharp intelligence."

"Be careful," said SheLa. "I warned you."

"You mean that, in fact, you are not thinking

of the meaning of life, but of the dress you will buy tomorrow on Fifth Avenue?"

"I mean," said SheLa, "that, for all you know, I *might* be."

"Good," said the Buddha. "You might be thinking about it. I *am* thinking about it. Here and now. I am imagining that I am you and that tomorrow I shall have all the dresses in Fifth Avenue to choose from . . ."

"Not all," said SheLa. "Some of them are much too expensive. I shall go to Saks. That," she said graciously, "is the name of a shop."

"Has this shop got a number of dresses?"

"Thousands."

"All different?"

"Not as different as they pretend. Dresses never are. But why do you ask?"

"Because I want to know if you will have any difficulty in choosing the right one."

SheLa clapped her hands. "Difficulty?" she said. "I shall have the shop down, and even then I may walk out without buying anything at all."

"Very well. I am imagining that I have those thousand garments displayed before me. Here," said Gautama, with a gesture, "is one. I reject it. It is too . . . too . . ."

"Go on," said SheLa.

[77]

"Much too . . ." said the Gautama, floundering. "Too big," he finished weakly.

SheLa laughed. "Never mind," she said. "You did your best. Let me take over. *That* one," she went on, screwing up her eyes, "is far too smart for me. I always say my *face* is chic. A little too chic. So I have to be careful."

"We reject this one, then," said Gautama. "We take up *this* one." He made another gesture.

"That one," said SheLa immediately, "is too fussy. I am feminine, but not fluttery. I have a direct way of talking. I must have a direct dress."

Buddha clapped his hands as though to a servant. "Take away the indirect costume. Bring a direct one."

" 'Simple' is the right word," said SheLa. "Yes. That one is simple enough. But it lacks a trick."

"How can a thing be simple and tricky at the same time?" said the Buddha with some irritation.

"How can a thing be This and not This at the same time, to say nothing of being This and That?" SheLa asked in reply.

"I surrender," said the Buddha. "Let us take another."

"Ah!" said SheLa. "Now that one is something different. I can see myself in that. It's me."

She paused, then said carefully, "All the same . . ."

Buddha intervened. "We shall assume that this is the dress you want," he said peremptorily.

"Bully!" said SheLa. "Why?"

"Because if we don't, I shall keep you up all night and, more importantly, because it exactly suits my argument."

"But will it suit *me?*"

"You said it would. You said it *was* you. Now," said the Buddha, "suppose, at the very moment that you said those words, you reflected that you, after all, were made up of sawdust like Ananda. Suppose you thought of the fact that all your choosing and all your study of your shape and your personality were no more than spinning words around something that was irrevocably settled for you at the moment of your conception in the womb —worse still, settled immeasurable aeons ago, when the dust first started on its myriad combinations. Would you really go on choosing clothes?"

SheLa picked up Ananda and held it in the air. "Could I, Ananda?"

"Could Ananda choose a bone?" said the Buddha.

SheLa slowly put down the dog. She laid it back on the pillow. She pulled up a sheet and covered it up to its neck.

"Mrs. Hammy Bits doesn't like dogs, so I make do with Ananda," she said slowly. "I pretend."

"Is pretending very satisfactory?"

"Yes," she said. Then, "No."

"With a toy or a dress, perhaps it might be," said the Buddha. "But, with the great moral decisions of living, it can never be. When this terrible thing that I have been describing is known to everyone, men will still pretend they are free, but they will know they are pretending. Then a languor will spread in the world, a lazy despair, a sad, sad frivolousness. You will be like children playing with toys for the last time, because you have grown too old to believe in them. What was high purpose will become a whim; boldness will mean no more than watching the play of chance; to try to be good will only be trying to be what you must be; to be bad will not matter because it cannot."

"Fate," said SheLa. "What about fate? That's an idea that's been around a long time and does nobody much harm."

"Fate is something you believe in when things are not going well. When they are, you forget it. This is something quite different. You can conveniently forget that you need air to breathe."

"Death," said SheLa. She reached out and put her finger on the bedpost. "Touch wood

[80]

quickly," she said. "It's an unlucky word." The Buddha obeyed. "Death," said SheLa again. "We've got to die, but we don't have to think about it all the time."

"Some men have done so," said Buddha. "And they have denied that it existed."

"That's an easy way out," said SheLa.

"It is a sublime way out."

"You mean that we ought to say this dust thing doesn't exist really? That it isn't true?"

"We must say that it cannot be true," said the Buddha.

"But that's pretending."

"No. Pretence is belief without passion. This belief must be filled with a passion which will carry mankind to the throne of God himself, protesting."

"Who would have that passion?" said SheLa.

"I had—once."

"But you're dead and gone to glory. If I said the Buddha came to me in suite sixteen in the Saint James' Hotel and said this to me, and the other to me, they'd think I was as nutty as Hammy Bits. You've had your day, you know. You're too familiar. Everybody knows what you said and what you think and very nice, too, thanks very much, *om mane padme hum*, if you'll pardon the expression."

[81]

"What you have said is quite unpardonable, but it is perfectly right," said the Buddha. "Nobody will listen to me. But they might listen to you."

"Me?" said SheLa, shocked. "Me? Talking sublime? I'm the last person anybody would choose to talk religion with, because it is religion, isn't it, that you mean?"

"Yes."

"Of course it is. It's your profession. But it isn't mine." She put her hand to her mouth. "Ooo!" she said. "But it is, isn't it?"

"It could be if you approached it with the professional seriousness that I do," said the Buddha.

SheLa got off the bed. She walked to the window and stood for a long time gazing at New York. Then she said, "It won't do."

"Why?"

"Hammy Bits. Mrs. Bumbling Hamilton Bitney and all her likes. They'll listen to me, all right. You're correct there. But just think of the nonsense they'll make of what I say. Just think of the nonsense they've made of what *you* said."

"Not in the beginning," said Gautama. "When I was on earth my disciples took me with deep seriousness."

[82]

"Well, that was a long time ago, wasn't it? And they were all men, weren't they?"

"Not all, but mostly."

"I'll bet the women weren't your favorite disciples."

"I barely noticed them. At one time I had ten thousand followers, and that calls for a lot of housekeeping."

"So you kept your females in the kitchen?"

"If I remember rightly, it was impossible to keep them out of it."

"There you are, you see. Things have changed. Women have the vote."

"I'm not proposing that we should run an election on the fate of the universe," said Gautama.

"Of course you aren't. What I mean was that nowadays women have a finger in the pie in everything—and not in the way they did in your kitchen."

"Then let us concentrate on the men."

"But you're forgetting something. Men run after women."

"Not all the time, surely."

"Well," said SheLa, "of course, they sometimes have to stop to catch their breath. But it means that, by and large, in the world today, women set the pace. Your world was a serious world. Ours isn't. It's not only the women who are scatter-brained, it's the men, too. They've got pretty things to play with, like motorcars and motorboats and all sorts of other gadgets. The women like to see them making fools of themselves, and the men like the women to like them. Men play silly women's games, like cards, and they take them seriously. They've learned to love a good old gossip, too. They huddle together over coffee and sandwiches and talk a horse's hind leg off. They call it having conferences. I've been to some —Hammy Bits made me go. They are nothing but an orgy of gossip, some of it pretty spiteful, too. The world's not serious any more, like it was in your day. There's so much to do. So much fun—if you think it's fun. If you don't, you're an oddball. Women don't like men who are oddballs. They can't understand them, and a woman likes to know a man as well as she knows the back of her hand. And no woman wants to be an oddball herself. She thinks all women who are original in their habits are starved of sex. Women laugh at Hammy Bits, and she knows it. She cries sometimes. But she's a widow, so it's not so bad—widows are allowed to be a bit funny. Besides, she's got five million dollars. No. It's no use. I can see what you mean. I can see what you want. But it won't work. Sorry."

[84]

SheLa looked out of the window. She yawned. "The dawn's coming up," she said. "I feel ever so sleepy. I'm sorry I'm so little help." She yawned again. "Maybe the other one will be better for you. The boy. The HeLama. Have you seen him?"

"Not yet."

"Why not try?"

"I shall. But I'm very disappointed," said the Buddha.

"Please don't be cross," said SheLa. "I feel bad enough about it as it is. And so, so, so tired. After all," she said, with a little wail, "I've just traveled I don't know how many thousands of miles and . . ."

The Buddha put out his hand. He touched her forehead. "I have been very inconsiderate," he said. "It is due to my living so much alone. I am grateful for everything you have told me, and I shall think it over very carefully. Now, my child, sleep, and sleep soundly."

SheLa drowsily nodded. She moved over to the bed. She got into it and pulled the sheets up to her chin. She was almost asleep." "Not cross with me?" she mumbled.

"Not at all."

She struggled to open her eyes. "Oh dear, oh dear," she said. "I shall wake up in the morning and I shall be furious because I met the Buddha and made a fool of myself."

"No," said the Buddha gently. "You will wake up in the morning and feel very happy because you have been a very good girl. Now go to sleep."

He stood watching her for a while. She opened her eyes once again. "Forgot . . . turn out . . . light," she said.

The Buddha smiled. Slowly the splendid aura around him faded. The room grew dark save for the dim light from the window. SheLa said, "Thanks," and fell soundly to sleep.

The Buddha sighed and returned thoughtfully to Nirvana.

The telephone rang beside SheLa's bed. It rang persistently until she turned over, stretched out an arm and picked it up.

"Good morning," said a voice on the telephone. "You desired to be called, Your Highness. It is seven o'clock and the outside temperature is sixty-four degrees."

"Eh?" said SheLa. "Oh yes. Is it? I mean, is it sixty-four already? Oh dear. I'm still asleep. I had a wonderful dream, a wonderful dream. The Buddha came and talked to me."

"You're welcome," said the voice, and rang off.

[86]

SheLa thought for a moment. "Ananda," she said. "I behaved like a silly chit. I talked a lot of nonsense. Ananda, are you listening? Ananda! Where are you?"

She searched under the pillow. There was no dog. She threw back the bedclothes. "Ananda! Ananda!" she said. "Where have you got to?"

A dog barked. SheLa listened. It barked again. Then Ananda crawled out from under the bed, wagging its tail. It made an ineffectual attempt to jump on the bed, then fell back on the floor, barking with excitement. SheLa bent down and picked it up.

"Ananda," she said. "So I didn't make such a fool of myself, after all."

PART

[4]

EVERYWHERE

[4]

HER HOLINESS HAD DESERVED HER PRESENT FROM
Gautama Buddha, as the following sequence of
events will prove.

Those with a political turn of mind may recall that an American ambassador, appointed to
the island of Ceylon was found to be unable to
remember the name of the Prime Minister of
that newly free, independent and democratic country. This caused surprise everywhere but in Ceylon,
where the people have for centuries taken pride in
having impossibly long names, this being a sign of
reputable birth as much as the names Cabot and

Lodge are in the States. Mr. Srimavo Bandaranaike took the matter with high good humor, died, and was succeeded by Mrs. Srimavo Bandaranaike, his wife.

Administrations also changed in the United States, but after a somewhat more elaborate process. As we have seen, the new President had developed the system of sending representatives to give him first-hand information about foreign countries. Before this idea was abandoned in favor of leaving it all to Trundle, one such man was sent to Ceylon. He met Mrs. Srimavo Bandaranaike and pronounced her name correctly, thanks to a lesson along Trundle's lines. This, however, was the only success he had. He wrote back a survey and had the embarrassing experience of being told by the Assistant Secretary of State himself that his report was a dismal disappointment. This was because the representative had devoted all the substance of his observations to the fact that the Prime Minister of Ceylon was of the female sex. He considered this very significant, not only for Ceylon, but for a true assessment of the way the Orient was going.

It was well known that the East was rapidly adopting Western ways. It was also well known that Western ways often did not seem the same when they had been adopted. According to him, here was an instance. The West had invented

women's suffrage, but (he said) he had never felt
that it was meant to be taken to quite such lengths.
Here in Ceylon, the extraordinary proposition that
a wife was as good as her husband and could, at
any time, step into his shoes was taken as an ac-
cepted fact.

While he was satisfied with Mrs. Bandaranaike's adhesion to the free world, he said he was dis-
turbed by the thought that the principle might
spread to other Eastern countries. He had gone to a
great deal of trouble to find out who were the wives
who would, in that case, take their husband's
place—and where there was more than one candi-
date, which wife was most likely to win the fight. He
had drawn up several tables in which wives were
designated in one column, W-1, W-2, W-3, and
concubines, C-1, C-2, C-3, in order of importance.
Their educational attainments were symbolized
in another (RW—read and write, X—illiterate,
and so forth) ; and, in a third, their probable align-
ment in the cold war (pro C, pro W, N, neutral,
B, blank on the whole subject, etc.) . It made grim
reading to him, but not to the State Department.
There this extraordinary document was subjected
to careful evaluation from which it emerged that
the representative had recently suffered a nasty
divorce and was mentally unbalanced on the subject of women. The report was invalidated, and sent

to the Buddhist desk, where William Weekly lost it.

We now come to the period of the two Dalai Lamas; the representative had proved right, at least in principle. Ceylon had a new Prime Minister, but once again she was a woman, the wife of a celebrated man who had run for office but at the last moment declared he was too old to take up the burden. His wife had stood in his place and had been elected without demur.

Ceylon is a Buddhist country. The new Prime Minister, as one of her first acts, had sent a cable to the Secretary-General of the United Nations asking that the matter of the two Dalai Lamas be discussed by the Security Council as a possible threat to world peace. She also asked her representative to introduce a motion giving Ceylon's full support to SheLa.

The Prime Minister of Ceylon had no strong feelings on the subject. But it was clearly a thing on which one could take sides and, being a womanly woman, she liked taking one.

The Secretary-General of the United Nations was a Buddhist himself. That being so, he did not wish to take action which might be thought precipitate. So he persuaded the Assembly to set up an investigating committee of nations of the Afro-Asian bloc, who would have a sympathetic under-

standing of the problem. When SheLa arrived in
New York, this committee was about to have its
first session. It awaited one member, as we shall
see.

Meantime, SheLa suffered a misfortune. She
barely had time to take one entranced walk down
Fifth Avenue when she was informed by the State
Department that they were moving her out of the
Saint James' immediately and to a private house on
Long Island. In future she was to stay at Beach
House, Quarg.

Behind this move lay a chain of events not
wholly dissimilar to those that had led up to the
U.N. motion. The principle mover here was
Mrs. Norton Bedford, a determined enemy of Mrs.
Hamilton Bitney since the time the latter had been
intolerably rude to her at a World Faith Unity Conference. This meeting was intended to find a common basis of belief in all religions. Mrs. Norton
Bedford had represented the Protestant persua-
sion, which she had every right to do since she was
a member of a great number of important committees in that branch of belief. She had made
some remarks about amateurs in the religious
field, when Mrs. Hamilton Bitney got up and said
that if she meant her (Hamilton Bitney), then she
would like to tell her that she (Norton Bedford)
was a professional. Mrs. Norton Bedford instantly

asked "a professional *what*, Mrs. Bitney?" to which
Mrs. Bitney should have replied (she meant to
but lost her head) "a professional member of religious committees," for Mrs. Bedford did accept
fees for her tireless service. Mrs. Hamilton Bitney
said, however, that she would leave *that* to the conference to decide, and the fat was in the fire. Matters were not improved subsequently by the fact
that both ladies lived in San Diego, Mrs. Hamilton
Bitney, as we know, for six months of the year, but
Mrs. Norton Bedford all the year round. Her residence in that place greatly strengthened her moral
fiber. She liked the climate. But she had observed
that the people who lived in equable and sunny
climates were generally lax in their behavior. She
thought this a pity. It spoiled a number of otherwise desirable residential areas, not only in the
States, but also in Europe and elsewhere. She determined to show by her own example that this need
not be so. Latitude, as she was fond of saying, was
only a geographical expression. So she sunbathed,
but only to fight the good fight the better. The good
fight, in this case, was to uphold the principles
that had built the United States of America in face
of the subversion of her co-citizen, Mrs. Hamilton
Bitney. The two women went at it, hammer and
tongs, wherever they could—at meetings, at fund-

raising tea parties, and even in letters to the press. On the whole, Mrs. Bedford prevailed.

Then Mrs. Bitney stole a march on her. Mrs. Bedford read of SheLa's arrival and installation at the Saint James'; she saw it was a time to do or die. She took the plane to Washington and saw Senator Staunch. An hour later she left him. The Senator was considerably shaken.

He, immediately, wrote a note to Trundle and had it delivered by hand. Trundle read it carefully, passed it on to his assistants, and quite failed to grasp its significance, as was his usual practice. He would have forgotten the matter if he had not visited Capitol Hill that afternoon and run into the Senator as Staunch was coming off the Senate floor. The Senator buttonholed him and carried him off to the refreshment room.

Senator Staunch was a tall, thin man in his early fifties. He had a well-modeled but rather long nose, and watchful manner. Above this nose rose a broad brow behind which, it was clear, considerable activity went on. His manner of address was obliging, but every so often he revealed, or rather flashed, a remarkable shrewdness which had taken him to the post of the Senate leader of his party, which was then out of office, but powerfully represented in both houses.

In the country, Senator Staunch was famous for his steady conservatism. He was as faithful to the principles which had made the United States as Mrs. Norton Bedford—but unlike her, he had made a thorough study of them, being a lawyer. Staunch's steadiness had become a legend. But Staunch was not a man to be deceived by his own public image. He regarded himself as a sound lawyer and a first-class politician. Early in his career, he had surprised his campaign organizer by turning down a slogan: "Staunch in name and staunch in deed." Staunch had said, "It won't do. It might win votes, but it'll ruin me in the Senate. That's not the sort of man they're looking for at all. The place is thick with pigheads already." He chose instead, "We want Ben Staunch." The electors did want him and, after some years, the Senate found it could not do without him. He was now a man of wide influence. Everybody on Capitol Hill liked dealing with Staunch, because Staunch got on with anybody who was ready to do a deal. Trundle would have liked to have dodged his invitation, but he knew that he dared not.

Senator Staunch ordered tea for himself, remarking that his constituents were always surprised that he drank so un-American a drink. Trundle replied that, in his academic years he had drunk rivers of it, and ordered some too. When it had brewed through the little tea bags to both men's satisfaction, they drank. Staunch saw he had put Trundle at his ease and off his guard.

"You've found the precedents I asked for, of course?" he said.

"Eh?" said Trundle, sipping his tea.

"The precedents," said Staunch.

"Ah," said Trundle. "Pass the sugar, will you?"

The Senator obliged. "I'm sure," he said, "that sometime or other the State Department must have entertained the head of a religious confession at the expense of the Government. They must have."

"Oh!" said Trundle. "Oh, yes. I mean, no. No precedent. Not that we can find."

"Not even," said the Senator, "the Papal Legate?"

"No," said Trundle.

"Well, then, the Archbishop of Canterbury. We must have given him the VIP treatment."

"Never," said Trundle.

"Or the top brass of the Orthodox Church. What's he called?"

"A Patriarch," said Trundle. "No. No Patriarchs."

"Then this Dalai Lama is the first to have the privilege?"

"Seems so," said Trundle.

Senator Staunch, watching him closely, noticed a certain offhandedness in his reply. The Senator judged it to be due to the aroma of the tea carrying Trundle back to faculty meetings where he had been the panjandrum. The Senator judged the moment ripe to hit Trundle over the head.

"Then Mrs. Norton Bedford is right. Putting up the Dalai Lama at the Saint James' at the public's expense is a clear violation of the principle of the separation of Church and State."

Trundle set down his cup forcibly. "I've never heard such damned nonsense," he said. "Who the devil is Mrs. Norton Bedford?"

"She's a woman who's just been to see me," said the Senator. "She can make a lot of trouble for people who need the Protestant vote. I'm sure," he said, "the President will see that."

He allowed Trundle time to digest this.

"But it's really very simple," he went on. "Couldn't you just move the lady in question out of the Saint James' and put her up in a private house? There's bound to be somebody ready and eager to put up the Dalai Lama and move out lock, stock and barrel to do it. Especially," he added, "in New York."

"It's impossible," said Trundle. "With a debate coming up at the U.N., the President would never agree to just dropping this girl flat. He couldn't. He's put his whole weight behind the idea, and the public . . ."

"George," said the Senator, "how long have you been in Washington?"

George told him.

"Well, George," said the Senator, "I've been here eighteen years. During that time, I've done a lot of studying. George, have you ever thought about the Constitution?"

George said he had.

"So have I," said the Senator. "And, to me, the most striking thing about it is that it won't work. Nobody can govern the country under it. If he tries, there's someone or something to stop him. The House stops the President, the Senate stops the House, the House stops the Senate, the Rules Committee stops everything except the trains at the railroad station. But in eighteen years I've discovered that it *does* work. The country is governed, George. How? I'll tell you. By mutual understandings, by compromises, by adjustments: in a word, George, by deals. For instance, very shortly the President is going to ask me to breakfast. It's a bad time for me. My digestion doesn't get going until ten o'clock. Never mind. The President is a busy man. I eat my bacon and I eat my eggs. But I'm in a gloomy mood. The eggs weigh on my stomach. Mrs. Norton Bedford weighs on my mind. So does the President's proposal in the Budget to continue the aid for schools—a very controversial point, that. But it's dear to the President's heart, and with all his responsibilities, we ought to help him when we can. *I'll* help him, too, if it's possible. And he'll need my help in the Senate. That's why he is giving me bacon and eggs. Sooner or later, he will say, 'Ben, you're looking worried. What is it?' And I'll tell him. He will offer to do anything he can. But I'll tell him it's difficult. I'll put your point to him, George. I'll tell him the way you feel. So there we'll be, back again, with this controversial thing about the schools on one hand and Mrs. Norton Bedford on the other. The President will say—"

" 'Trundle again,' " said Trundle, staring into his teacup, but so softly that the Senator could barely hear him.

Then Trundle looked up. "Very well, Senator. I'll do what I can, sir."

"I knew you would," said the Senator as he rose, and he spoke the truth.

Trundle's tea with Senator Staunch took place at four o'clock on a Thursday afternoon. Fourteen hours later a similar light collation was being served in the capital of the United Patriotic Independent

Fan Republic, in West Africa, where it was eleven o'clock on Friday morning. It might be said that, compared with Washington, it was always morning in the Fan Republic. Instead of the tired atmosphere of Capitol Hill, here all was fresh and forward-looking. The Fan Republic was young. It formed part of the new world of Africa and Asia which has opened new horizons in our thinking. Here were the new men, unfettered by old shibboleths, who were aware that the destinies of mankind might one day be in their hands, men who, at world council tables, were already shaping history.

One such unfettered man was Mpongwe—unfettered in mind and unfettered in body since the Day of Liberation when his loyal shock troops had defeated the forces of his opponent M'trombo and, pausing only to eat the usurper's Chief of Staff, had released Mpongwe from the filthy prison into which his rival had flung him.

President Mpongwe, at the time I have stated, was taking coffee with young M'bo. It was a signal honor. M'bo was only twenty-six years old. Slim, nervous, with the boldly undulating nose of the Fan people and their wide, expressive eyes, M'bo was an attractive representative of the younger generation. He was much liked. He had expected a brilliant career, but his first post had exceeded his hopes. One short year after receiving his doctorate from London University, he was to be the new Fan representative at the United Nations. That was enough. But this morning his cup ran over. President Mpongwe had invited himself to coffee in the young man's rooms. M'bo nervously adjusted his framed parchments on the wall for the twentieth time, tightened the knot in his tie and dusted the ultimate speck of African dust from his London suit. The coffee was on the boil on the gas ring. There was nothing more to do except to wait for the ceremonial ritual of a Presidential visit to begin.

He did not wait long. In five minutes he heard the sound of the Presidential armored car. Soon after came the squealing brakes of the Presidential escort of jeeps, then the sound of the Presidential honor guard dismounting and forming up. M'bo composed himself by the door as best he could and awaited the final ceremony. Immediately it came. The sergeant of the guard pounded rhythmically on the door with the butt of his submachine gun, shouting, "Open up, open up." M'bo was moved. This was the way the President was always announced. It was a custom hallowed by association with the stormy days of the foundation of the Republic. M'bo would treasure the dents on the wood for years.

M'bo flung open the door. Pushing aside the sergeant, the Fan Republic's man of destiny came into M'bo's modern apartment, holding out his hand with democratic affability. M'bo bent to take it, not from servility, but because President Mpongwe, apart from his other gifts, had a regal fatness and shortness. Among the populace, he was known as "Nga," an affectionate and respectful nickname which may be translated as "Floppy bottom" (the people's speech is racy). It was an allusion to the fact that he had regally-sized buttocks which would, in the bad old days, have hung down on either side of the Royal Stool—a propitious sign.

Of course, Mpongwe would have none of this nonsense. Once asked if he were not of royal descent, he remarked that he was a man of the people. "No descent: all ascent," he said; and the words were inscribed on the base of the statue in front of the jail into which he had been thrown. He wore no sign or symbol of his authority. He was dressed in a crumpled white suit and dirty white sneakers. Such was the man who now, without ceremony, sat down in one of M'bo's simple chairs.

The sergeant sniffed loudly.

"I shall be some time," said the President, with that touch of thoughtfulness which he never lacked. "Tell the guard to stand at ease."

No words were needed. The sergeant thrust

his head out of the doorway. He spat out some brown saliva from the tobacco he was chewing. The guard of honor, with a cheer, flung down their automatic weapons and squatted on the ground. The sergeant closed the door and squatted down himself inside M'bo's room.

"Let us speak English," said the President. "That fellow sitting there is brooding over his pay. I don't trust him."

"Willingly," said M'bo. "Can I offer Your Excellency some coffee?"

"You jolly well can," said Mpongwe, speaking in the precise Bloomsbury accent of University College, London. "I'm parched."

The coffee was served. "Sit down, boy, sit down," said the President. He greedily drank some coffee. He looked at a gold chromometer set with brilliants on his wrist.

"Eleven o'clock," he said. "Coffee. Just like the lower refeck, eh, M'bo? Just like the old days."

Tears came to M'bo's large dark eyes. The President had referred to the custom in the College of going to the lower, or basement, refectory to take coffee in midmorning and to discuss everything from progressive sex to the future of Africa. Much of modern history was shaped there and at the similar institution in the nearby London School of Economics.

"Did you go there?" asked the President.

"Always, sir," said M'bo.

"I bet you cut lectures to do it, just as I did," said the President expansively. "Whom did you cut? Never mind. We all did it. No shame in it. Though I must say I have sometimes regretted one or two. I remember Brogan. D. W. Brogan. Did you read political theory with him? No, you couldn't have. He'd gone up in the world by your time. Brilliant young fellow, he was. Witty. Poor devil. We didn't know he was going to be a big gun. We cut his lectures without mercy. He felt it, I think. He used to take one look round the rows of empty chairs and rub his spectacles with his fingers till they were all smeared and he couldn't see through them. Then he used to give his lecture. His favorite topic was the Constitution of the United States. I attended one lecture on the presidency. Wonderful. Brilliant. Incisive. It changed my life. I've modeled myself on the American President, you know. I'd like to meet him and tell him so. There's a job you could do for me, M'bo. Drop a word."

"Oh *yes*, sir," said M'bo. His whole face glowed. He had been given an affair of state to discharge by this incredible man, and within three brief minutes.

SheLa

"In my time, it was all Laski, Laski, Laski.* But as for me, I preferred Brogan. Cooler. More collected. Laski was friendly towards Africans, but I always felt he wanted to lift us up to higher things. And, after all, what had he to offer. John Stuart Mill and Karl Marx. Mother's milk and vodka. It wasn't to my taste. The others worshiped him. But to me he always had a touch of the missionary about him. Looked like one, too. Not that I'm against missionaries on principle. Be careful about that when you're in the States. Every faith is free to practice its rites in this Republic. They can make conversions, too, provided the convert applies for a government certificate which will be used purely for statistical purposes. Make a mental note of that, M'bo."

But M'bo's student habits asserted themselves. Seizing pencil and paper, he wrote out the advice in full.

"Good," said the President. "You can't be too careful. You'll be asked questions about it all over the States, especially if you get caught in one of those color-bar incidents."

There was silence for a while, as M'bo wrote and the President drank coffee.

* Professor Harold J. Laski (1880-1948), influential writer and lecturer on political theory, sometime professor of the Chair of Political Philosophy, London School of Economics.

Then came the sound of distant fire from sub-machine guns. M'bo put down his pencil. He looked at the President. The President looked at the sergeant.

There was another burst of fire. "Sergeant," said the President, "I thought I gave orders . . ."

"Brr . . . brr . . . ratatat tat," said the sergeant, grinning. He couched his weapon in his arm and, waving it, made the noise of firing it. He grinned widely. "Protestants."

The President stirred his coffee. "Where's Colonel O'Shaugnessy?"

"Hunting," said the sergeant.

"Hunting what?" said the President.

"More Protestants," said the sergeant.

"If that wild Irishman doesn't make up his mind to obey my orders, I'll break him," said the President in English to M'bo.

There was another burst of fire, then silence.

"Spies, of course," said M'bo.

"Good boy," said Mpongwe. "That's a thing I'd like to discuss with the President. He and I have constitutionally the same concentration of powers in our hands. But I wonder if he has the same troubles as I do. Unreliable aides, obstreperous military. I've no time to read the newspapers, but I bet he does. I'd like to talk it over with him, President to President, man to man. Still," he said, "that's enough about my problems. I'm here to talk about yours. Speak up, my boy."

"Well, sir," said M'bo. "You mentioned those color-bar troubles. What would you recommend, sir, as a course of action?"

"A picnic basket in the back of the car. It's so simple I can't imagine why it hasn't been thought of by the others."

"They weren't *you*, sir," said M'bo.

"Maybe not. Thank you, my boy. I appreciate your compliment. Though I say it myself, I'm not a fool, or I wouldn't be where I am. Any idiot can govern a country which obeys the police. It takes brains to rule a people who eat them. Your coffee's getting cold. Drink up and let's have some more."

M'bo picked up his cup. He raised it shakily to his lips and then set it down again.

"What's wrong, boy?" said Mpongwe. "Oh, I see. I mentioned eating—no, no, no, I won't go on," he said soothingly. "I see the topic worries you. Make a note and remind me before I go to put you in the picture about it."

M'bo took up his notebook and wrote. To cover his confusion, he rose, took the coffee percolator off the stove, and poured more coffee.

"Splendid," said the President. "Excellent coffee, upon my word. Tell me, M'bo, how do you feel about this new job at the United Nations?"

"It's a great honor, sir."

"Have you studied the organization?"

"Yes, sir."

"What do you make of it?"

"Well, sir, first and foremost it *has* helped to keep the peace."

"Wherever," amended Mpongwe, "nobody has thought it worth while to start a real war. But how do you look on the job from your own point of view? What is your aim in life, M'bo?"

"I want to be a diplomat, sir."

"Good," said the President. "Then address the General Assembly as often as you can."

"I shall, sir."

"It's wonderful practice. There's nothing like having to tell lies in front of a hall full of people who are being highly paid to do exactly the same thing. And serve on as many committees as you can. By the way, I've a little surprise for you."

The President fumbled in his jacket pocket and brought out a crumpled sheet of paper. He smoothed it out and passed it across the table. "This came this morning. It's a message from the Secretary-General. It says that the representative of the Fan Republic has been selected to serve on the— What's it called?"

M'bo, in a bewildered voice, read out aloud;

"The Committee of Investigation for Tibetan Religious Affairs?"

"What do you know about Tibetan Religious Affairs, M'bo?"

"Absolutely nothing, sir."

"Excellent. Try to stay that way. It's the great secret of being a successful neutral. If you understand what's going on, a bright young man like you is bound to take sides, and then bang goes our foreign policy. Abstain from voting on anything, even if they ask you to say whether the earth goes round the sun. The Independent Fan Republic stays firmly neutral until somebody takes notice of us."

"I understand, sir. But—excuse me—when I address the General Assembly, what shall I say?"

"Say that the Fan Republic is determined to resist colonialism from whatever quarter it may come."

"Oh *yes*, sir," said M'bo, "with all my heart."

"Um," said the President. "And just between you and me and the gatepost, if some colonialism doesn't come our way pretty damn quick, I won't be able to pay the army—and both of us will be out of a job."

"I'm not sure I quite follow, sir," said M'bo.

"Never mind, my boy," said the President genially. "You can leave higher policy to me." He put down his cup. He rose to his feet. "Well, I must be going," he said. M'bo had risen, too. The President linked his arm in his.

"Good luck, my boy," he said. "Don't forget my advice and—yes—one last thing. See America. It's a great country. It's got a lot in common with the Fan Republic. It fought and won its freedom, and George Washington could no more trust his army than I can. It went home at harvest time, you know, just as ours does. And go to Washington. See the Constitution at work. It's one of the noblest inventions of the human mind. The men who drew it up had the same problems as I have had— a lot of warring tribes, none of which were really prepared to give up a jot of their independence. God knows, I hope Fan common sense will stop short of civil war. But not even Abraham Lincoln could avoid it in America. Go and see them in their own homes, boy. Talk to the housewives. You'll feel at home. You'll find you might be talking to your own mother. They've got the same aspirations as our own Fan people—a refrigerator, a car and two square meals a day under the belts of all the family. Don't talk books or art or music or any of that—any more than you do when you go back to your own village. You'll find the same homey atmosphere, provided you don't put on side. Do as you would at home. You won't be expected to take off your trousers, but take off your jacket. And don't have one skin too few. If you do come across an American who won't dine next to a Negro, remember that we dine off 'em."

He reached the door. The sergeant shambled to his feet. The President regarded the soldier for a moment with distaste. Then he turned back to M'bo.

"That reminds me that I promised to deal with that little problem of yours before I went. You're bound to be told that there are some battalions in our glorious army that have been known to consume their prisoners. It is true, M'bo. Quite true. With the greatest reluctance, I was forced to use such men as my shock troops. It was a terrible weapon, M'bo, and one that would make any civilized man hesitate before using it. But they were my shock troops. They brought the war with M'trombo to an end a year before the carnage would have stopped otherwise. I meant to disband them. But M'trombo has formed six battalions of them and I know he means to use them. In the interests of humanity, I am prepared to sit down at the conference table any day he chooses and agree that this terrible threat should be removed forever. But he must have the interests of African civilization as sincerely at heart as I have. Until then," said the President, and a broad smile spread over his generous features, "the gastronomic shield must remain, in the national interest. Make a note of what I said. Goodbye now—and don't forget to arrange that meeting with the President. He and I have so many problems in common." With that, he went.

Much at the same time, a third collation was being served, and, since the place was Peking, it consisted of tea. The tea was poured into porcelain cups but otherwise there was no ceremony. Nor was there any display of fine manners. The guest was Tschempko, famous as we know for his rudeness, and the host was Wang, a man ruder, if anything, than Tschempko. Wang was at this time the Chinese Minister for Foreign Affairs but, as he was saying in a loud voice, "Our trouble is we haven't any. For years now, the Americans have worked an extremely clever plan by which six-hundred million people are totally ignored. I am Minister for Foreign Affairs and I have nothing on my desk but border squabbles with the Indians—a lazy, idle lot of corrupt politicians who sit picking their noses and jiggling their legs at every conference we have with them. Their only interest in a quarrel is whether or not it will help them to line their pockets."

"That is merely vulgar," said Tschempko. "I

have been to India. Some of their top men have very high ideals. It may seem strange to us, but nonviolence—"

"Making money on the stock exchange is a very nonviolent business," said Wang. A tall and athletic man of fifty, his face was as smooth as Tschempko's was rugged. It gave him an added insolence.

"I don't blame them," said Wang. "The whole country fell into their laps like a ripe plum. Millions of plums. The population is docile and when it isn't the police rapidly bash a few heads in and all is quiet again except for the ticker tape. But I'm not here to discuss the Indians, and neither are you. Our business is with the Americans, and in that quarter our patience is exhausted. I am convinced that if some woman hadn't written a novel about us, the American people would not know we existed. We've fought 'em. Remember that, Tschempko. Fought 'em in the field, which is more than the Russians have ever done, in spite of your bluster. We fought them in Korea and what happened? The American newspapers called it the Forgotten War. Two of the mightiest peoples of the world were locked in a bloody combat and one paper ran the same communiqué for a week on the front page to see if anybody would notice. Nobody did. When you were having your highly successful circus over Berlin, I personally drafted a statement in which we said that if the Americans dropped nuclear bombs on us, we were quite ready to lose sixty million and not turn a hair. It was a statement so outrageous that Genghis Khan, dead drunk, would have blushed to make it. What happened? Nothing. I'm told that in Washington the cocktail set said, "Ah yes, yes, well, but sixty million *Chinese*."

"I never heard that remark," said Tschempko.

"You never heard anything," said Wang. "I'll bet you never even mentioned us. Well, that's at an end. We intend to take up this Tibetan business and play hell with it."

"But," protested Tschempko, "it's such a trivial affair, a foolishness . . ."

"No more foolish than bombarding Quemoy on the odd days of the month—and *that* is what we have been reduced to."

"But you speak of the American people. You don't know them as I do. You can't move them without a great moral issue."

"Did you have that in Berlin?" said Wang.

"Certainly not. But we were lucky. We were going along quietly, expecting nothing but a series of get togethers, when Trundle took a hand. It was he, you know, who thought up the idea that Berlin was an outpost of freedom. My Number One told me himself that when he first heard of it he couldn't believe his ears. We'd had trade fairs for years in East Germany at which we positively begged industrialists from all over to take space; we'd even had an American exhibition in Moscow. And here was Trundle saying that Berlin was a shop window which had to be defended so that our people could press their noses against it. It was luck. Pure luck. And of course it worked. To tell you the truth, we just sat with our mouths open, watching. At one stage, they were going to mobilize Europe. If they had gone ahead with it, Italy would have voted Communist at the next election, without a doubt. Togliatti told me personally that he was furious. You know how hot-tempered the Italians are. He said that you couldn't found a revolution on a fatheaded blunder. He said he felt it was a lifetime's work being thrown away."

"Still," said Wang, "it worked."

"Like a charm," said Tschempko. "Of course, when it got to atom-bomb shelters, we saw the thing had got out of hand, and we all let it cool down. Though heaven knows, I've got my work cut out keeping it from boiling up again—and who knows, it might still. Yes, it worked. But you can't expect Trundle to turn up with a brilliant idea for us every time we flick our fingers. He's a busy man."

"So am I," said Wang, and looked at his watch.

"Then you are determined to go through with this plan?"

"Fully—and a dozen others. But this one here and now."

"But," said Tschempko, as near pleading as he could manage, "the moral issue. Where is it? And the American public insists on it. Look at the time the Old Man took off his shoe. Not a ripple. Why? There was no issue of right and wrong in threatening to throw your footwear about. Then again, it's confusing. The Dalai Lama is Buddhist. That's a *religion*. How can we explain to the American public that we, as atheists, support a religious figure?"

"How do you explain the Patriarch of Moscow?" said Wang.

Tschempko was silent.

"It will save time if you do not treat me as a child," Wang continued.

Tschempko sighed. "What do you want us to do?"

"Present the true Dalai Lama to the United Nations and expose this bitch who's been put up with American money."

"You want us to take him over there?"

"Yes."

"Who'll pay? You know how stingy the Old Man is about foreign junketing."

"You can keep it austere and simple."

"A private visit, eh?"

"Yes. With the utmost publicity."

"We could put him up in the country," said Tschempko. "That would be cheaper. There's a house we've bought on Long Island as a rest center."

Wang took up a pencil. "Where?" he said.

"I never can remember the name," said Tschempko. "Something Red Indian."

It was, of course, Quarg.

Tschempko rose to go. He sighed. "How I'll convince the Old Man about this, I don't know. I'm already in hot water about allowing the President to score off me."

Wang gave him a patronizing pat on his shoulder. "You might find it easier than you think. I'll tell you a secret. Do you know what your boss said to me after the last Party Congress?"

"No. He doesn't confide in me."

"He said, 'Wang, I've come to the conclusion that the Chinese are the most pigheaded people on earth.' That's what he said, Tschempko. His very words. And he was quite right. Anyone could have discovered the same thing by reading our history. But who does? *Who* reads it? The longest recorded history in the annals of mankind, and who in the West can guarantee to answer five questions about it?"

" 'Pigheaded,' " repeated Tschempko appreciatively. "Say what you will about the Old Man, he's got a pithy way with words. Well, sir," he said, and sighed again, "I'll not take up more of your time. Goodbye." With that he shook hands and left.

PART

[5]

QUARG

[5]

THE BUDDHA AND THE DEVIL WERE ONCE MORE TO-
gether inside the white fence of Nirvana. The Buddha sat beneath his tree. The tree was a tranquil
blue.

"A charming gesture," the Devil was saying.
"A most charming gesture."

"What?" said the Buddha absent-mindedly.

"The dog. Bringing the dog to life," said the
Devil. "If the remark will not offend Your Highness, I always thought you were far above such
human touches."

"I trust I am not above a simple courtesy.

Considering I burst into her apartment in the dead of night, the young lady was extremely forbearing with me. To leave her a little present was the least I could do."

The tree glowed a deeper blue, and the Devil, noticing it, said, "Certainly I have never known Your Highness to be in such a good mood."

"Mood?" said the Buddha. "I don't know that I'm in any sort of mood whatever. I am simply . . . simply . . . well, fascinated. I have found the world so full of surprises. Take that young man, for instance, the other Dalai Lama."

"Yes," said the Devil. "Tell me about him."

"I appeared to him in Lhasa. In the Potala itself."

"At night?"

"No. In the morning, when he was alone and saying his prayers in front of an idol. It was a very debased work of art. I assumed the same position in space as the image and, if I may say so, I greatly improved its appearance. I spoke to the boy."

"Was he frightened?"

"Not in the least. No more than the girl. It took him a minute or two to make sure that I was really the Buddha, and then what do you think he said?"

"I cannot guess," said the Devil.

"He said, 'So you're the Buddha, are you? I

always thought there was something in it, though not very much.' " In that single phrase this Tibetan stripling dismissed three thousand years of religious speculation."

"You were angry, of course?"

"Not at all," said the Buddha. "I could not have put the thing better myself. I immediately decided that this was the person I was looking for to tell the truth about the preposterous joke which is being played on us. I told him the gist of the matter. He thanked me for the information, but said he wasn't on the biological side. He was more interested in physics. He said his one ambition was to be sent up in a rocket. Apparently his advisers had held out hopes of something of the sort, if he'd be a good boy and do as he was told. Tell me, what is an astronaut?"

"An astronaut is a person who flies in outer space," said the Devil. "It is part of a collective madness which seized the human race after their last global war. I would be glad to tell you about it because it is much on my conscience."

"Proceed," said the Buddha.

"On your way to the earth, you may have noticed a number of tin cans of various shapes circling rapidly around the globe. These contain dead dogs, dead monkeys, dead rats and dead men. This repulsive museum is currently regarded as the ultimate triumph of the human genius. Some of these tin cans bear the symbol of one country, others bear the symbol of its rival. When one country, at great expense of effort and treasure, contrives to send a tin can aloft, the other country feels itself bound by national honor to send a similar one or, if it be possible, one that is heavier and bigger. The ultimate object of this competition is to land a living man on the moon. Since a reason must be found for such folly, it is maintained that the country which first lands a man on the moon will win the next war. This is so silly that not even soldiers and sailors and airmen believe it, although usually they will believe in anything which will make the public spend money on them. Nevertheless, they are forced, from fear and cowardice, to exert all their efforts on this . . . this . . ." The Devil paused, searching for a word.

"This lunacy," the Buddha supplied.

The Devil nodded in agreement. "And never," he said, "has the word been more aptly applied. As I have told you, it has been my aim during the whole of my dealings with human beings to urge them to rise above themselves. As the story has it, it was I who tempted Eve and subsequently Adam to eat of the fruit of the Tree of Knowledge. I have, until now, been proud of what I did. Observing these canisters circling the globe, I am more and more convinced that the Creator knew what he was doing when he put the Tree under a ban."

"He could very well have kept it under a ban," said the Buddha. "You, after all, are only a creation of his whim."

"I would gladly argue that point with Your Highness if only the times were more propitious to philosophy. And allow me to say, sir, that I have always regarded your majestic and daring speculation as my greatest triumph, for without me no human being—as you once were, Your Highness—would have dared to question the workings of Creation."

"I do not admit your premise," said the Buddha, "but continue."

"When you walked the earth and taught your sublimities, my hopes for the human race knew no bounds. Even when it turned away from your teachings and began exploring the nature of the dead and living things around it, I still hoped. Yet —here we are. The human race has discovered the way that matter is put together and is busily using its knowledge to blow itself apart. Faced with having to save the earth from destruction, it turns its back on the problem and strains every nerve to reach the moon. And now, as Your Highness' incomparable intelligence has divined, it is about to unlock the last secret of life. There will be nothing left for human beings to find out. You, sir, believe that with the explanation of the universe in their hands the human race will rise to the final triumph of facing its Maker as an equal. Would that you were right, Your Highness. For my part, I have no such confidence. The joke, sir, is more subtle. It is this. The bigger the things that he lets them do, the pettier their minds will grow. They will perform actions worthy of Gods with the intentions of nincompoops. Almighty God will have perfected a race of almighty fools."

But the Devil is the father of lies, and the lie he told the Buddha about the small-mindedness of all of us was soon nailed to the counter. The events in Quarg are a part of history. They brought, it is true, the world to the verge of war. But to look on the black side of things is to play the Devil's game. Here we shall emphasize the qualities of statesmanship, the breadth of vision and the sense of responsibility to the destiny of the human race that averted the catastrophe.

When Trundle left the Senate after his meeting with Senator Staunch, he was a dispirited man. He walked disconsolately three times around the Folger Shakespearean Library, giving way to a nostalgia for the old days. He had not an idea in his head, and in his academic career these moments had been golden. It was then that he would summon the faculty and, with a characteristic broadness of mind, throw the whole problem on the table for discussion. His penetrating handling of the ideas that emerged had won him good opinions from all, including those with whom he ultimately, reluctantly, disagreed, because they could not withhold their respect from so impartial a man.

Now he had no one to summon but his aides, and they were useless. The course of international events had shaken their nerves too badly. Trundle, and Trundle alone, would have to act. He turned his back on the Folger Library, squared his shoulders and determined to model himself on the remarkable man who sat in the White House. He would be dynamic. He would telephone somebody. The question was, whom? Back at his desk, he stared disconsolately at the papers in front of him, feeling the difference between being a man of decision and being just Trundle.

Then a sheet from a scratch pad caught his eye. On it was written the name of Mrs. Hamilton Bitney. In a moment the solution to his problem formed in his brain. He would persuade Mrs. Hamilton Bitney to insist that her protégé be removed from the Saint James' Hotel. For religious reasons, perhaps. Or for something else. The thing was not to hesitate, but to *telephone*.

He got through to the Saint James'. Mrs. Hamilton Bitney, when she had got over the excitement of being telephoned from the White House, proved most obliging. She had been feeling, she said, for some days that Her Holiness should move to a quieter place and one, Trundle gathered, where Mrs. Hamilton Bitney would not be on the floor below in a room inadequate to her position as Her Holiness's inventor. Mrs. Hamilton Bitney went on to say she owned a most suitable place—a house on the Long Island beach, at Quarg.

Her Holiness and her suite moved there, as inconspicuously as possible, the very next day. The house was long, low and commodious. Room was found for everybody and, since she owned the place, Mrs. Hamilton Bitney ruled the roost. Reporters were forbidden and, in fact, after a day or two none came. This was because, in the rush of great events, SheLa was forgotten.

Mrs. Norton Bedford had tasted blood. Church and State were once more as separate as she could wish. The country was no longer footing the bill at the Saint James', and it only added to her pleasure to think that this was being done by the impertinent Mrs. Bitney. Hard upon the heels of her triumph came news which once more roused Mrs. Norton's desire to fight for the right. The news of Colonel O'Shaugnessy's shooting of Protestants in the Independent Fan Republic filtered through Mpongwe's censorship and made headlines across the whole of the United States.

Mrs. Bedford saw Senator Staunch. Senator Staunch saw the Secretary of State. The Secretary of State, swearing he would have the liver and lights of anybody in the Department who told Trundle what was going on, saw the permanent delegate to the United Nations. A motion for information was tabled and young M'bo found himself on the podium, defending his country. He was brilliant and utterly loyal. His youth added conviction to his masterly speech, in which he defended Mpongwe and laid the whole blame on O'Shaugnessy.

M'bo left the rostrum to thunderous applause. The Afro-Asian bloc joined with the Communists in condemning colonialist interference in Africa. The United States' delegate found himself in the position of having either to withdraw his own motion or having the Communists vote for it *en masse*. He exerted himself manfully in the corridors of the United Nations. He pointed out that O'Shaugnessy was an Irishman from Clonmel, and

Ireland had never had any colonies. In the resulting confusion he found an ally in M'bo, who in the hope of getting another chance to address the Assembly, agreed to support a motion for the adjournment of the debate.

Mrs. Norton Bedford saw Senator Staunch. Senator Staunch had breakfast with the President. The President asked him what he had on his mind. Senator Staunch told him, but then he met his match. The President refused to be budged. He told the Senator roundly, over the bacon and eggs, that he would do nothing at all in the matter until a full, independent fact-finding inquiry had been made.

The Senator mentioned the Protestant vote.

The President mentioned the Irish vote.

The Senator said the Protestants were demanding action.

The President said in his position he had to take the broad view.

The Senator said nothing. Privately he was relieved. He felt grateful that a man of decision and character was at the helm.

The breakfast proceeded smoothly. At a subsequent press conference, the President stuck to his guns. Half the newspapers in the land were baying at his heels, but they did not alter his decision. The country discussed the matter with passion for a whole week.

In Peking, Wang lost his temper. Enraged at finding the whole question of the Dalai Lamas dismissed in favor of what he called a squabble in the African undergrowth, he demanded that Moscow take instant action along the lines that he had arranged with Tschempko.

The Kremlin reluctantly told Tschempko to take action. The young Dalai Lama was flown to New York. Little interest was shown in his arrival, but news announcers, impartially covering the events of the day, showed pictures of his arrival, these being clearer on the television screens than the two blurred photographs of O'Shaugnessy (one taken when he was twelve, the other more recently) which had been their staple for six days.

HeLama was taken, as had been arranged, to the embassy rest house on Long Island at Quarg. It was a long, low, commodious house on the beach. It was separated from Mrs. Bitney's house by approximately four hundred yards of sand dunes and nothing else.

SheLa was sitting in front of the television set in her bedroom. There was nothing to be heard in the room save the sound of the waves on the beach. SheLa, in her dressing gown, was watching the pictures as they flickered silently on the glass screen. Every so often, she straightened in her chair and turned her head as though listening. Ananda, the dog, lay curled up on the bed. It was dreaming and from time to time it squeaked. When it did so, SheLa said, "Sh . . . Sh." Soon the television went blank. SheLa switched it off and took up a book which she stared at for a while without reading it.

There was a tap at the French windows. Then another, and another. SheLa jumped to her feet. Ananda woke and growled. SheLa ran to the dog and held its muzzle so that it could not bark. Ananda wagged its tail. When she was satisfied that the dog understood it must make no noise, she left it, went to the French windows, and opened them.

A young man stepped into the room. He was curiously dressed in an opulently embroidered blouse that was tucked into a pair of blue jeans. On his feet were slippers decorated with gold thread. Once in the room, he took SheLa in his arms and kissed her long and passionately. Ananda sat up, wagged its tail violently.

They made a handsome couple as they stood embracing. The boy was slim. His complexion was the same glowing brown as SheLa's, and his hair was black like hers but short. His long eyelids, now closed in pleasure, were exquisitely shaped.

SheLa pushed him away gently. "Joe," she said, "I thought you would never make it."

"Trust me," said Joe, and kissed her again. "I've never failed yet. I'm late tonight because they sat around yap-yap-yapping about politics. I have to wait till they're all in bed and snoring before I can get out of my bloody skirts."

"Jeans suit you," said SheLa. "Are you hungry? I've saved something from supper."

The boy shook his head. He took SheLa's hand and drew her down to the couch. He sat beside her and said, "We've got to talk. Tonight's the night."

"How do you mean?" said SheLa.

"I'm not going back."

"You mean *ever*?" said SheLa, in consternation.

"*Ever*," he said. "I'm through. I'm finished with it. It's all washed up. I'll never put another skirt on in my life. I've done with being the Dalai Lama for good and all."

"Joe!" said SheLa. "You mustn't. You can't. Oh, Joe, just think of the riot this is going to cause."

Joe folded his arms and composed his boyish face with an expression of manly determination. His name was not Joe, for he was the HeLama, and was called by a composite name made up of seventy-four holy syllables. SheLa called him Joe because, like so many of the younger generation in the East, she was thoroughly fed up with everything Oriental.

HeLa got up. He strode round the room. SheLa watched, torn between dismay and admiration for his figure in blue jeans.

"Look," said HeLa. "I love you."

"Yes, Joe, and . . ." SheLa stopped.

"I've loved you ever since I saw your picture in the papers. I've loved you ever since I saw you on television. I've loved you like crazy every night I've come through those windows. You're the most beautiful girl I've ever seen."

"You haven't been allowed to see many," said SheLa.

"Never mind. I've seen heaps and heaps of pictures in magazines and they're all hags compared with you. I never imagined that there was anybody in the world like you, and there isn't. Besides, I can't keep away from you. I think about you every minute of the day. I'm going to marry you."

"But Joe," said SheLa. "That's not the way to propose. You might at least ask me if I love you."

"I won't," said HeLa, "because you'll say you don't just for the sake of argument."

"Yes, Joe. I do say things for the sake of argument. It's a bad habit. It makes me sound like an old maid."

"That's something you'll never be now," he said, and sitting abruptly on the couch, he took her in his arms and kissed her.

Afterwards, SheLa said, "But, Joe, you're just a boy."

"I'm nineteen."

"But I'll be twenty-one in April," said SheLa.

"So?" said HeLa. "Where's the great difference?"

"Not now, there isn't," said SheLa. "But just think. When I'm forty-one," she said, and made it sound immeasurably old, "you'll still be in your thirties."

"I'll be the father of three children and that'll put years on me," said HeLa.

"Oh," said SheLa, "so you've got it all worked out?"

"Of course I have. What else do you think I've been doing all these days? Listening to that claptrap about the cold war? No. I've been thinking and thinking about our life together."

"Have you thought what we're going to do for money?" said SheLa.

"Yes. First we'll elope, and then we'll ask for asylum here in the States."

"On what grounds?" said SheLa. "You've got to have grounds."

"Religious persecution," said HeLa. "What about the Pilgrim Fathers?"

"Ye . . . es," said SheLa. "That's quite good. But have we been persecuted?"

"What the hell do you call what we've been put through?" said HeLa violently. Ananda barked and SheLa said in alarm, "Not so loud."

"Sorry," said HeLa. "How I hate all this secrecy and whispering."

"So do I, " said SheLa. "But you haven't told me what we shall do for money."

"I shall advertize for a job."

"Oh, Joe!" said SheLa, and giggled. "How will you advertize? 'Dalai Lama, well-trained, seeks position as. . .' As what, Joe?"

"Damn all Lamas," said HeLa. "I shall advertize: 'Young man, healthy, active. . .' "

" 'Handsome,' " said SheLa.

" 'Willing go anywhere, do anything.' "

SheLa took his hand. "Joe," she said, "will you really go anywhere, do anything?"

"Yes."

"For me?"

"Yes."

"Only me?"

"Only you."

"*With* me?"

"Always."

SheLa said, "Joe. Kiss me, or I shall be silly and cry."

Later, pushing her hair back in order, she said, "The old bitch might give us some money to start off with."

"She could afford it," said HeLa. "What with five million dollars."

"Oh, she's got more than that. Much more," said SheLa. "She's not the fool she makes herself out to be. Do you know what, Joe? Once she went to see Mahatma Gandhi, and the old man said to her, 'There's no use your talking to *me*, Mrs. Bitney. I haven't a rupee to my name. Millionaires can only talk to other millionaires.' So he gave her an introduction to a cotton magnate called Birla, and the Mahatma was right. The two got along like one o'clock, and Hammy Bits has been quietly making millions ever since. It's in cotton. Nobody's supposed to know. I could blackmail her."

"What's blackmail?" said HeLa.

"Something a nice boy like you should leave to his wife," said SheLa. "Besides, it might not be necessary. She's got a heart somewhere or other inside her. She was quite reasonable over Ananda."

The dog, hearing its name, jumped off the bed and came towards them. HeLa patted it.

"Joe," said SheLa. "He came to you, too, didn't he?"

"Ananda?"

"No. The other Ananda. Him."

"Yes," said Joe. "Nice old man. But like all old men, he thought that all young people were just dying to do exactly what their elders did when *they* were young. So we didn't hit it off."

"Were you afraid?"

"Not a bit."

"Funny, isn't it?" said SheLa, putting her head on his shoulder. "We both of us took it so calmly. I suppose it's like being the children of famous actors. You get used to big moments. Joe, when are we going to run away together?"

"I've run away already. I'm not going back. I told you."

"But where will you sleep?" said SheLa.

"Here."

"Oh, but you can't," said SheLa.

"I don't mean *here*," said HeLa, blushing. "I mean in this house."

"But where?" said SheLa.

"Haven't you got a private chapel and all that rubbish?" said HeLa.

"Yes," said SheLa. She got up, took a key from the dressing table, went to a door and opened it.

"Does anybody ever come in here?" said Joe, coming up beside her.

"No, never. I make a terrible scene if anyone tries. I have to have some privacy and Hammy Bits agrees."

"Well, then," said HeLa. "It's settled. I sleep in there."

"I'll get a blanket and a cushion. You'll have to sleep on the floor," she said, and began stripping sheets off her bed. She made a huge bundle. HeLa took it from her. He gave her a quick kiss.

"My," said SheLa, "*what* a scene there's going to be when all this comes to light."

SheLa was the brains of the elopement. She searched in her handbag and found enough money to pay for HeLa's fare on the railroad to New York. She stole into Mrs. Hamilton Bitney's study, found a timetable, and noted that HeLa would have to leave the house before six to be sure to catch the first suitable train—one that would arrive in New York when it was light, so that HeLa would not be too confused. From the railroad station, he was to ask his way to the Saint James' Hotel, where he was to take a room. SheLa said that they would be sure to give him one because they had always been such polite and helpful people when she had stayed there.

In the meantime, she would tell the whole story to Mrs. Bitney, after Hammy Bits had stood on her head—when, as SheLa said, she was always in a good mood. SheLa would then join Joe at the Saint James' with the money. She found Joe an overcoat in the locker used by Mrs. Bitney's Negro butler, and all was ready. HeLa went into the chapel to get some rest before his exertions of the following day.

SheLa slept fitfully. At twenty minutes to six, she woke him, and after a last long embrace he slipped quietly out of the house. He walked to the station, bought his ticket and waited, shivering in the cold morning air, for the train.

As he waited a heavily built man in a dark suit went to a telephone booth and dialed a number. The heavily built man, keeping an eye on HeLa through the glass, said into the receiver, "Chief?"

"Yes?"

"Burton."

"Yes, Burton?"

"He's been on the tiles again."

"Who? Bonzo?"

The chief of that department of the New York City Police which attends to the security of visiting diplomats was a heavy reader. He had coined this code name for the male Dalai Lama from a reminiscence that Buddhist priests were once called bonzes.

"Yes, Bonzo. Through the usual window into the girl's room."

"I'll make a note of it. But remember what I told you. They're U.N. people, sort of, and we've got strict instructions to keep our noses out of anything dirty connected with the U.N. Foreigners are foreigners, and they have their ways. So keep our Romeo and Juliet's little games under your hat."

"Yes, sir," said Burton.

" 'Bonzo, Bonzo, wherefore art thou Bonzo?' " said the Chief.

"What, sir?" said Burton.

"Never mind. It's Shakespeare."

"Oh," said Burton. "I thought you said 'Where for?' It's New York. I was behind him when he bought the ticket."

"What ticket?"

"For New York. Bonzo left Beach House at five forty-five this morning and made for the station in an overcoat with the collar turned up, blue jeans and Oriental-style footwear. He was alone. He bought his ticket and is now waiting on the platform."

"Holy Mother of God," said the Chief. "We can't have that at all. Alone, you say?"

"Yes, sir."

"Is he running away?"

"He has that look about him."

"Keep with him. I'd better get on to Security at the Soviet Embassy. And Burton. . ."

"Yes, sir."

"Just keep with him. For heaven's sake, take no action until we know where we stand."

"No, sir. Very good, sir," said Burton. He rang off. The train came in, and unobtrusively he followed HeLa aboard.

HeLa was looking out of the parlor-car window at the stupendous spectacle of New York as it rose over the flats. The train had stopped at a station. Two men came quickly down the center aisle and one of them put his hand on HeLa's shoulder. HeLa jumped to his feet. He swung the bucket chair round against the legs of one of the men and bolted down the car. But they caught him by both arms. As they hustled him off the train, HeLa shouted "Help! Asylum! Refugee!" But, as he shouted in Tibetan, nobody understood him. Burton heard all, and saw all, but bound by his orders, he made no move.

In the car, HeLa sat in silence all the way back to Quarg. At Quarg, still in silence, he went to his room. One of the two men stood outside in

the corridor, the other on the sand path that ran
by the window. HeLa stood by the window a whole
hour, listening to the comings and goings and tele-
phonings and looking across the dunes to SheLa's
window. At long last, she opened the shutters.
She waved her hand and then turned back into
the room. A servant closed the shutters, and they
were not opened again all day.

Since the two Russian officials had undoubtedly abducted HeLa from the train, the Soviet
Embassy immediately issued a statement accusing
the United States of having abducted the Dalai
Lama. By noon, the news was in the papers and on
the radio. By three o'clock, three of Mrs. Bitney's
servants had sold their information to the Soviet
officials who now thronged the rest-house. By the
evening, the whole story was told in an Embassy
statement.

By threats of violence and blackmail, the
statement said, the henchmen of the false Dalai
Lama had induced the true Dalai Lama to visit
Beach House every night for approximately a week,
where he had been mercilessly interrogated. On the
night of the abduction, he had been seized and
locked in a small airless room. He had managed,
however, to escape, in an overcoat belonging to
one of the staff. Terrified that he would be fol-

lowed, he had made for the railroad station in order to put as much distance between himself and his persecutors as possible. An alert security agent, on duty at the station, had telephoned the Soviet Embassy, which had immediately sent two officials in a fast car to catch the train at the first possible point. There they had rescued His Holiness and brought him back to Quarg in safety. His Holiness was in a state of nervous prostration as a result of his harrowing experiences.

Trundle was immediately informed of the true facts of the case by the New York Police. The President, in Miami, suggested that Tod be called, since romance was his line. Tod wrote a warming statement about HeLa's love for SheLa and her response to it through all the barriers of the cold war. The State Department submitted it to Weekly, asking if it might offend religious sentiment, and when Weekly said it might— on the grounds that almost anything that one could imagine might be offensive to religious people— the Department vetoed the whole idea. The Department drew up a statement of its own, toned it down to meet Weekly's point, sharpened it up to get the propaganda value of the abduction, worked it over to please the neutrals, cut it down to avoid offending the U.N.—and then canceled it entirely, until the whole situation had undergone careful review.

Twenty-four hours later, Soviet-employed workmen had erected a barbed-wire barrier all around the house at Quarg, and the crisis began.

The State Department instantly denounced the barrier as a gross violation of diplomatic privileges. The Soviet Embassy replied with what, to the State Department, seemed an unnecessarily large quantity of photographs of United States embassies all around the world with barbed-wire protection, and even temporary walls, erected in times of riot.

The President summoned Trundle for a chat. The President was on his yacht. The President was suitably attired. So was Trundle. As Trundle came up the gangway, he saw the President at the top.

"So the press gang got you, did they?" said the President, with a sunny smile; and it was in that happy mood that the rest of the day was passed. Only once was the subject of Quarg mentioned, during a pause in a shuffle-board tournament.

"George," the President said, "this is a small thing, but we've got to watch it. It's the sort of thing that rouses the State Department. It's a breach of protocol, there's no doubt about it. But this country has a long tradition of ignoring protocol. Remember the time when our ambassador turned up at the Court of St. James in trousers instead of breeches? It did no harm to the King of England. And a bit of barbed wire will do no harm to the United States of America. Still, we must watch it. Your partner's signaling to you, George. It's your turn at the board."

Trundle, with a grateful smile, crossed the deck and poked a shot at the numbered squares. It roused a wail of despair from his partner. But George had played with tears in his eyes. Who but the President could have taken so vast a view of things?

Unfortunately, the next day was a Sunday and, to make matters worse, it was a fine day. Tens of thousands of New Yorkers streamed out from the city on to Long Island to look at the barbed-wire entanglement. Beach House was surrounded by a great throng of sightseers, held back by a cordon of police. From time to time, on the advice of the authorities, SheLa came out and walked in the garden. A superb press photograph of her was taken, with her head thrown back and an intense look in her eyes. It was printed the next morning with the caption *Breathing Freedom's Air,* but, in fact, SheLa had been gazing desperately in the direction of the other house in the vain hope of seeing Joe.

The President, as was his habit, had judged the mood of the people correctly. While he relaxed on his yacht, the sightseers held picnics on the sand dunes. All was happy and bright, in direct contrast to the shuttered windows and grim defences of HeLa's prison.

But next day, the mood of the city and, in due course, the mood of the nation drastically changed. A reporter on one of the more popular New York papers had written an account of the day. Reading over his copy, he realized that what he had written, though true, lacked impact. One of the difficulties was the matter of names. SheLa's residence was called Beach House. But the Russian one had no name at all. The reporter invented one; he called the whole area—house, grounds and barbed-wire perimeter—"The Red Beachhead."

The dry-goods merchants and other suppliers in the nearby town of Southport were the first to rise to the occasion. To a man, they refused to deliver food or anything else to the Russian outpost. This drove the Embassy officials to do their own shopping. There was, therefore, a constant coming and going of men carrying bags, each of them relentlessly watched by the television and other cameras that now encircled the house. An anxious country, watching the images of these suspicious individuals coming and going at all hours of the day and night at the Red Beachhead, demanded why the Federal Bureau of Investigation was not taking action. Thereupon the FBI encircled the outpost with detectives who, over the violent protests of the Embassy officials, searched the bags. They found nothing but victuals, but the practice of bringing in supplies by hand stopped. Instead, the Embassy sent in a truck twice a day carrying the necessary provisions.

The next day a detective inspector of the Bureau stopped the truck and, abruptly opening the back door, searched the vehicle. Nothing was found, but the Embassy instantly lodged a protest with Washington. The truck, it appeared, was, in fact, the diplomatic bag, duly sealed, and thus immune from search. The State Department rejected the protest and Moscow recalled its ambassador for consultations. Washington did likewise.

The Secretary of State acted swiftly. At a press conference, he admitted that a technical violation of the immunity of the diplomatic bag had been committed, but he resolutely stood by the State Department's rejection of the Soviet note of protest. He maintained that the rejection concerned the tone, not the contents of the note. At a cocktail party in Moscow, the Soviet Premier remarked to the assembled diplomats, "They admit to stealing our horse but don't like us shouting 'Stop thief!'" In reply, the Government of the United States ordered a second barbed-wire fence to be built thirty yards beyond from the one built by the Russians. All visitors to the house were compelled to pass through a check point.

This measure satisfied the nation for some forty-eight hours. But a violent altercation broke out between a policeman and an Embassy official who was submitting his identity papers at the check point. The official broke away and ran across the dunes between the two wire fences. The policeman followed him, drawing his revolver to fire a warning shot. Unluckily, he tripped over a clump of grass and fell headlong. The admonitory bullet, instead of going up into the air, shattered a window in the house.

Thirteen American Embassies behind the Iron Curtain had every pane of glass shattered methodically by protesting mobs. Wang ordered Quemoy to be bombarded with unprecedented fierceness.

Then the news broke in Peking that the policeman's bullet had killed the Dalai Lama. Wang ordered general mobilization and gave Formosa twenty-four hours to surrender.

The Pacific fleet weighed anchor, and the

armed forces of the United States were put on a general alert.

Wang was thus the winner. The subsequent conferences between the great powers were rendered continually sensational by Wang's truculent speeches. There was no war, not a shot was fired except that of the policeman, but his had echoed around the earth. Peace, when it came, owed nothing to either the Russians or the Chinese, but everything to the President's masterly handling of the situation. It was he who suggested that the United Nations be asked to place a peacefully armed contingent of men in the no man's land between the two fences—where, of course, they still are. The Russians evacuated their house, although still claiming its immunity. HeLa went with them, having been quite unharmed during the whole proceedings.

PART

[6]

IN NIRVANA

[6]

THE BUDDHA AND THE DEVIL WERE ONCE MORE talking in Nirvana. The tree under which the Buddha sat was as tranquilly blue as the sky after a storm.

"If it hadn't been for your penetrating commentary on what was happening," said the Buddha to the Devil, "I would really have been quite alarmed. I thought nothing could save the human race from blowing itself to bits, and, faced with that prospect, I found I had a deep affection for the preposterous creatures. Are you sure things have quieted down?"

"It depends on what things you mean," said the Devil.

"Quarg," said Buddha. "I saw it all, you know, with my own two eyes, on my own two feet. I was quite unnoticed. Nobody thought it strange that a rather elderly Buddhist monk should be among the spectators."

"The Quarg crisis is quite forgotten," said the Devil. "The only question that remains is which side shall be the first to take down the barbed wire. A mixed commission has been set up to decide. So far it has had one hundred and thirty-two meetings without result, and it will probably have one hundred and thirty-two more. Meanwhile, all that there is to report is that the wire has grown so rusty that it will probably fall down of its own accord."

The Buddha stared into space.

"Your Highness is thoughtful," said the Devil.

"It is my nature to be thoughtful," said the Buddha, shortly.

There was silence in Nirvana for a while. Then the Buddha said casually,

"That little dog I made seems to be a healthy animal. I heard it barking away in the house. For a moment I thought I would go in, but I changed my mind."

"She has still got it with her," said the Devil. "Would you like to know how she is, or would I be disturbing Your Highness' meditations with trivialities?"

"SheLa is the reverse of trivial," said the Buddha.

The Devil was silent.

"I am not meditating," said the Buddha. "You may go on."

The Devil was still silent.

"Has she married the boy?" said the Buddha at last.

The Devil smiled. "No," he said. "No. As she always said herself, there is something of the spinster about her. Perhaps that is why she views women with such a cold eye. When Hammy Bits —I beg Your Highness' pardon—when the Hamilton Bitney woman learned of the romance she flew into a jealous rage. SheLa has left her. Mrs. Bitney has set her up in a shop just off Fifth Avenue, where she designs and sells Oriental trinkets. Her shop is called 'SheLa' but hardly anybody can remember what it refers to. The boy has disappeared."

"It would seem that the Americans have very short memories," said the Buddha.

"The whole world has a short memory," said the Devil. "And that, perhaps, is a mercy in an age of futilities. If any human could recall all the collective idiocies that had taken place in his own lifetime, he would go out of his mind. Besides, they always have a good excuse for forgetting. In this case, all the talk is now of O'Shaugnessy."

"Ah, yes," said the Buddha. "I read about him. He shot Protestants."

"He went on to shoot Mpongwe. Then he took over the Fan Republic and is now setting up a black Empire in Africa. M'bo is his Minister of State for African Unity. So many Irishmen are emigrating there that it is being called the first Irish empire. I could go on . . ." said the Devil; but the Buddha said, "Thank you. That is quite enough."

The Devil rose. "Then I must be going," he said. "Besides, I see you have another visitor. If I am not mistaken," he said, shading his eyes and looking into the surrounding sky, "the Archangel Michael is winging his way towards you."

The Buddha rose. He took the Devil's hand. "Goodbye," he said. "I am grateful for all you have told me. My excursion back into the world has been made most instructive by your wisdom. My mission was a failure, but . . ."

"Your Highness should not blame yourself for that. It could not have turned out otherwise. I am informed that the laboratory in England where they are making the final steps in the discovery of the secret which concerned Your Highness has been declared a security area. It is thought that the discovery may have strategic implications. The world will now, undoubtedly, fling itself into an orgy of the usual nonsense. There will be a furious race to breed the first perfect Russian, the first perfect Chinese and, a little later, the first super-perfect American. And since everything will be clamped down under military secrecy, practically nobody will know what they are talking about. Your Highness, farewell."

He bowed. He unlatched the gate. He walked away and, as he did so, the Archangel Michael with a flurry of his great wings landed beside Nirvana and drew himself up into a military posture. The Devil went on his way. Michael followed him with a long look.

"Michael," said the Buddha. "Come in. Come in. It seems so long since I last saw you, but then so much has happened."

"A pleasure, sir," said Michael. "I am glad to see you back." He knocked on the fence.

"Ah, so you've remembered," said the Buddha. "I'm afraid I was rather short tempered when you last visited me. But there's no need of formality now. Are you on an official mission?"

"Yes, sir," said Michael. He unlatched the gate. He stood at attention.

"Allelu . . ." he began. Then he stopped. "I beg your pardon," he said. He went outside

Nirvana. "Alleluia!" he repeated. "The Commander-in-Chief sends you his best compliments, and
says that he would consider it a pleasure and a
privilege to meet you personally for a thorough exchange of views on any topic that you may have in
mind. The Commander-in-Chief wishes to make
clear that he expects and welcomes criticism."

The Buddha did not reply; instead he put
his hands behind his back and took a pace or two
across the fenced space of Nirvana. He stared down
into the sky below it. Still staring downwards, he
said, "Tell your Master that I thank him for the
invitation. I have waited a long time for it to
come. Now I have decided to wait some more before I accept it. Tell him I have still some thinking
to do before I meet him. Perhaps a great deal of
thinking."

He unclasped his hands and looked at Michael, smiling. "That is the end of the message,
Michael," he said.

"Very good, sir," said Michael.

"And now," the Buddha said, cheerfully, "if
I remember, you were partial to a certain bottle of
wine I had with me. Come in and sample some
more."

"Thank you kindly," said Michael, taking off
his helmet. "I will, Your Highness." He came in
through the gate, and together they sat down under

the tree. The Buddha produced the bottle and Michael, first raising it in salute, put it to his lips.

"Ah!" he said, and wiped his mouth with the back of his hand. "Just as good as ever."

"Have some more," said the Buddha. Then he added, "Looking back on our last meeting, Michael, I suppose you're rather surprised at my reply to your Commander-in-Chief?"

"Not really, sir," Michael said. "Of course, being a military man, I can't say I've got a great respect for the civilian side, as a whole. But the Devil —well, sir, he's an exception. *There's* an angel that knows his job and does it. I'd be a happy man if I had a few officers like him. No, sir, I can't say I'm surprised. Your reply is right in the routine, as you might say, sir."

"What routine?" said the Buddha, looking at Michael intently.

"Well, sir, it sometimes does happen that someone of exceptionally powerful intelligence wants to give the C-in-C a piece of his mind. Put the Chief to rights, as it were. And that's where the Devil does his drill. I've watched it many times. I didn't actually see the time he did it with the apple, but *that* story's got the gist of the thing."

Michael took a swig from the bottle. "Very smooth it is, too, sir. He begins softly; butter won't melt in his mouth. He raises your curiosity. Eggs you on. *Apples* you on," he said, and gave a soldierly guffaw. "Then—attention! eyes front!—and he gives you a good straight look at what human nature really is. And *that* gives you something to think about for a long, long time."

The tree behind the Buddha changed from blue to a dull red. "Michael," said the Buddha, and his voice caused the delicate leaves of the tree to tremble. "Do you mean to tell me that the Devil has had the blazing impudence to tempt *me*? ME?" said the Buddha, and his voice was thunder.

"Speaking out of line of duty, sir," said Michael, "yes, sir. That does seem to be about the shape of it."

The tree grew scarlet with the Buddha's rage.

A NOTE

A NOTE

THE BUDDHA'S SECRET BEGAN TO BE KNOWN among scientists—and laymen like myself who keep an eye on their doings—in the middle of the fifth decade of the twentieth century. In 1959, I published a book (*The Fig Tree*) which, in the form of a story, indicated one of the things we could at the time expect.

But even while I was writing, research had progressed far beyond my imaginings. On Monday, January 15th, 1962, the New York *Times* described the state of affairs in the following admirably clear words:

"In its quest for understanding the chemistry of life and the basic mechanism of heredity, whereby all things living reproduce themselves in their own image, the science of biology has reached a new frontier, said to be leading to 'a revolution far greater in its potential significance than the atomic or hydrogen bomb.'

"The latest discoveries on this new frontier were reported recently by Dr. Marshall W. Nirenberg and Dr. J. Heinrich Matthaei, of the National Institutes of Health at Bethesda, Maryland. In their pioneer experiments, which have opened a new era in the study of the living process, they have succeeded in partly cracking the 'genetic code,' the key of the reproduction of all things living.

"Their discovery marks the latest significant step forward in the understanding of the role of the two key chemicals that have been found in recent years to serve as the 'master-builders' of life, known as DNA (deoxyribo-nucleic acid) and RNA (ribo-nucleic acid).

"DNA has been identified, in one of the great discoveries of all time, by scientists at the Rockefeller Institute as the substance of the genes. The genes are the many thousands of units of heredity inside the chromosomes, the rod-shaped bodies inside the nuclei of all living cells. It is the genes, namely the DNA in a great variety of chemical patterns, in the fertilized eggs of all higher forms of life that determine whether the egg—a single microscopic cell—will develop into a mouse, an elephant, or a human being, or whether the fertilized human egg (ovum) will be born a Newton, a Beethoven, an Einstein or just an ordinary human being, or even an idiot.

"The DNA, in turn, creates RNA. Each type of DNA creates a specific type of RNA, in which it implants a 'genetic code' carrying specific instructions for creating one of the thousands of enzymes. The enzymes, in turn, carry instructions to synthesize the great varieties of proteins that constitute the multiplicity of organs and tissues of all forms of life.

"It is this all-important genetic code implanted by the DNA in the RNA that the scientists in the National Institutes of Health have partly deciphered. Their experiments have revealed that each of the twenty building blocks of the proteins, known as amino acids, is carried to the potential protein molecule, composed of thousands of amino acids, by a specific type of RNA.

"The great mystery still remaining is how the different RNA's are instructed by the DNA to carry their specific amino acid 'bricks' in the proper sequence. In other words, the genetic code still remaining to be deciphered is how the various types of proteins, such as liver, kidney, muscle or brain, all composed of amino acids but differing greatly in the number and in the sequence of their amino acid constituents are synthesized by the RNA.

"Both the DNA and the RNA are made up of chains consisting of thousands of simpler constituents, named nucleotides. These nucleotides, in turn, are made up of simpler substances, named purines and pyramidines, combined with a specific sugar and phosphoric acid.

"DNA and RNA differ only slightly in chemical composition but they are enormously different in their biological role. RNA contains the sugar named ribose, which contains five carbon atoms, instead of the six in common sugar. DNA contains another form of sugar named oxyribose, which has one oxygen atom less than ribose. In addition, DNA differs from RNA in that its nucleotide contains a different pyrimidine.

"It was learned in earlier experiments that the DNA first synthesizes an intermediate, the messenger RNA, to convey genetic information to certain specific structures, the ribosomes, present in both the nucleus and in the cytoplasm fluid surrounding the nucleus. The messenger RNA makes contact with the ribosomes and is believed to be incorporated with them, thus emplanting on them its code of genetic information.

"Following this, another recently discovered form of RNA, named S-RNA, goes into action. The S-RNA activates amino acids, there being a specific form of S-RNA for each of the twenty amino acids. Many types of S-RNA have been isolated and separated in recent months.

"Both messengers RNA and S-RNA are composed of the same nucleotides, combined with ribose, but they are very different in the sequence of their nucleotides. The messenger RNA is literally made in the image of the DNA of the nucleus.

"It is the role of the S-RNA to deliver its sporadic amino acid to the ribosomes, after they have been incorporated with the code-carrying messenger RNA. It is this specificity of the S-RNA that was proved experimentally by the N.I.H. scientists.

"These discoveries, Nobel Prize winner Anre Tiselius warned recently, if misused 'will lead to methods of tampering with life, or creating new diseases, of controlling minds, of influencing heredity, even perhaps in certain desired directions. This can result in a still more refined and perhaps still more dangerous way of abusing the results of research than that implied in the instruments of mass destruction.' "

Meantime *Nature*, the leading scientific journal of England, had announced on December 30th,

1961, that four Cambridge scientists had found the key to the genetic code. The year 1962 opened with reports circulating on both sides of the Atlantic giving the triplet codes of seventeen out of the total of twenty amino acids.

We have not long to wait. But then, when it comes, I suppose we shall all be so busy that we will barely notice it.

A. M.

Rome, Spring 1962

ABOUT THE AUTHOR

Born in London in 1912, of an Indian father and Irish mother, Aubrey Menen was educated at University College. Here his writing talent was discovered by the late H. G. Wells, among others, and led to a position as a dramatic critic and as director of the London Experimental Theatre.

Visiting India at the outbreak of World War II, Mr. Menen spent the next few years there broadcasting pro-Allied publicity, and became one of the leading personalities on Indian radio. Subsequently he was appointed to the Political Department of the Government of India. Since 1951, Mr. Menen has lived in Italy, where he has written a series of novels, essays and studies in history which have brought him a wide readership in America, Europe, and the Far East. When not writing, he travels extensively.

Mr. Menen has said: "At fifty most satirists start to mellow. I don't believe this has happened to me. . . . As a satirist, my desire is to amuse, rather than reform. Many of the world's tragedies have stemmed from people who have thought that human nature could be improved. . . . The message of at least one kind of satirist is that human nature is corrupt, but that this is not necessarily either a disastrous or a melancholy thing. . . ."

SheLa is Aubrey Menen's eleventh book.